GOOD SPORTS

A Bag of Sports Stories

Also available by Tony Bradman,
and published by Doubleday:

A STACK OF STORY POEMS

By Pat Thomson, and published by Doubleday:

A POCKETFUL OF STORIES FOR FIVE
YEAR OLDS
A BUCKETFUL OF STORIES FOR SIX
YEAR OLDS
A BASKET OF STORIES FOR SEVEN
YEAR OLDS
A SACKFUL OF STORIES FOR EIGHT
YEAR OLDS
A CHEST OF STORIES FOR NINE YEAR
OLDS
A SATCHEL OF SCHOOL STORIES

GOOD SPORTS!

A Bag of
Sports Stories

COLLECTED BY
TONY BRADMAN

illustrated by Jon Riley

DOUBLEDAY

LONDON · NEW YORK · TORONTO · SYDNEY · AUCKLAND

TRANSWORLD PUBLISHERS LTD
61–63 Uxbridge Road, London W5 5SA

TRANSWORLD PUBLISHERS (AUSTRALIA) PTY LTD
15–23 Helles Avenue, Moorebank, NSW 2170

TRANSWORLD PUBLISHERS (NZ) LTD
3 William Pickering Drive, Albany, Auckland

DOUBLEDAY CANADA LTD
105 Bond Street, Toronto, Ontario M5B 1Y3

Published 1992 by Doubleday
a division of Transworld Publishers Ltd

A catalogue record for this book is available from the British Library

ISBN 0 385 402325

Typeset by Chippendale Type Ltd, Otley, West Yorkshire.
Printed in Great Britain
by Mackays of Chatham, PLC, Chatham, Kent.

CONTENTS

GOOD SPORTS
A Bag of Sports Stories

WHO'S IN GOAL?

by Rob Childs

Got a few minutes?

OK, let me tell you what's been happening to our soccer team at school this year. We've been getting thrashed, that's what. You know, five or six goals and more put past us most matches.

If you ask me, it's mainly 'cause of these two boys in my class, Danny and Tom, right. Both nutters about goalkeeping, they are, real head cases.

I mean, according to my dad, you have to be a bit bonkers to want to play in goal in the first place.

'All goalies are crazy,' he says when he sees one of 'em on telly go diving down, teeth first, to grab the ball off all them flying boots. 'Well known fact is that.'

He's probably right too, if Danny and Tom are anything to go by. They're well crazy, I can tell you, and I should know. I've had to watch them all season trying to outdo each other and prove who's best.

1

I reckon it's more a case of who's worse. Even Stubbsy – that's our teacher, Mr Stubbs – can't seem to make his mind up. He just gives 'em half a game each instead and then it's a toss up to see who drops the most clangers. To stand any chance of winning, our team has to score more goals than we keep giving away at the other end.

Take that cup match last month, for instance. Danny let three daft goals in before half-time and actually had the cheek to look surprised when Stubbsy took him off. Amazing. You'd have thought he'd got used to it, but they never learn, neither of 'em. They both think they're the world's number one goalkeeper, despite the fact they're about as much use between the posts as a bust clothes line.

As soon as Danny had pulled off the team's bright yellow goalie top, Tom snatched it out of his hands. 'Right, you're gonna watch a real keeper at work round here now,' he boasted stupidly.

We went and lost 7–4, would you believe. Tom was soon upside down in a muddy puddle missing a skidding back-pass, and after that things just slithered from bad to worse. He trudged off the pitch at the end covered in long black streaks and Danny was waiting for him, gloating.

'Hey, Tom!' he cried out so we could all hear. 'I can sure see you've been working. You look like some dirty great big bumble bee.'

They prize this yellow jersey as if it was made out of gold. Mind you, it is pretty snazzy, I have to admit, and I've often quite fancied trying it on myself. It's got this large black figure one, see, stitched on the back, with padding across the chest and shoulders for extra warmth. Not that either of them two will ever get cold wearing it, the way they go charging madly around the penalty area, throwing themselves about all over the place just to show off.

They used to be good pals at one time apparently, until this pig-headed goalkeeping feud started. Now they refuse to speak – apart from insulting each other of course – and always have to be on opposite sides in practice games and kickabouts so they can both play in goal. They go berserk if you don't let them.

Even when old Stubbsy insists they play out on the pitch for a change, they just sulk and mooch around till he gives in. Trouble is, nobody else wants to go in goal anyway 'cause of all the aggro they get when they let one in. Danny and Tom, though, don't seem to notice. They're too busy arguing between themselves and blaming their defence to bother about what other people are saying.

It's no wonder we're in deep relegation trouble in the league. Well, I say *we*. What I really mean is our school, South Millington Primary. I've not yet played for the team, although I've been going to all the practices this season and watch most of the games.

'C'mon, the South!' I always find myself cheering. 'C'mon, get stuck in, fight for the ball.'

All sorts of silly things like that, you know, echoing what Stubbsy is shouting from the touchline. It's never any use. We end up crying out, 'Bad luck, South,' or 'Never mind, keep your heads up,' and 'You can still do it,' when we're about 6–1 down. Hopeless.

You must think I'm hopeless too, if I've not been able to get into such a rubbish team. Well it's not quite as simple as that, but you're not far wrong, I suppose. I can't control a ball properly or kick it very hard. I duck out of the way rather than do a header and my tackling's not much good either. But at least I'm keen to join in as best I can and Stubbsy's happy enough to let me, I'll say that for him. He always praises me up when I do something right.

The others tend to laugh at me a bit sometimes, but I don't really mind. They're OK, most of 'em, and I'm sure they don't mean too much by it. They know I can take a joke.

But even if I can't kick a ball very well, one thing they all agree I'm good at is throwing it. They often let me take the throw-ins when the ball goes out of play and I'm careful not to do any foul ones so they won't go changing their minds.

'You take it, Alex,' somebody'll shout. 'C'mon, throw it to me, down the wing.'

I'm willing enough to do that, right, as long as I can have a good run round with them and have the odd swipe at the ball when it comes my way by mistake. I just love playing football, I guess, even if I do have to put up with a bit of mickey-taking about it.

But with Danny and Tom, like I said, it's playing in goal or nothing. They only enjoy it when the other one gets beat and hate it when the same thing happens to them. Talk about being as sick as a parrot, as footballers always seem to say on the telly. The number of goals this pair see fly past them, their poor Pollies must live at the vets.

And when I actually managed to score one last week, I probably put Danny's into intensive care. He went completely bananas 'cos it was me. Totally flipped his lid.

Didn't help of course that Tom was cackling away at the other end like some demented witch. Danny knew he'd never be allowed to forget it, even if, for once, it wasn't his fault. I kept trying to say it wasn't mine neither. It wasn't deliberate or anything – unfortunately. The ball just hit me on the knee and deflected in.

Typical! My first ever goal and I couldn't even celebrate. I mean, it wasn't that I was scared of what Danny might do to me, but no goalie would think much of one of their defenders punching the air in delight after notching up an own goal!

Instead, I had to put up with him giving me a mouthful after he made sure Stubbsy wasn't around. Not that all the swearing bothered me, I can shrug that off, but what really hurt was him spitting out that I had no right to be at the practice in the first place.

What's that got to do with him? I've got as much right as anybody, and at least I know how proper footballers should behave during a match. Not like them two. You ought to hear the way they try and put one another off when they get fed up hanging around as sub.

They were up to their usual tricks again last Saturday morning, right in the middle of a vital relegation game. I was standing nearby when Tom came up to lean on the post and began to taunt Danny about my goal, starting one of their silly arguments.

'Fancy letting Alex beat you like that. You couldn't even stop a bus, never mind stop a shot!'

'Belt up!' Danny snapped, turning his back on the game. 'You can't even keep quiet, never mind keep goal.'

'Oh yeah! At least I can catch a ball. You can't even catch your breath.'

'Rubbish. You can't even hold your breath. Or your tongue.'

'Watch out!' I screamed, but by the time Danny glanced back round it was too late. Another shot was on its way to bulging our net and we were 2–0 down.

Tom's smirk was as wide as the gaping goal. He didn't care about the team. He was obviously just happy that he'd made Danny look stupid and that he'd be sure now to go on himself after half-time. Probably reckoned he could pull off some brilliant saves and end up the big hero. Ha! Some hope. If Tom was that good, he'd have been on from the start.

Somehow, there was no further score till it was his own turn in goal. Trying to be flash, he pretended to go the wrong way for a shot at first but

when he dived back full length to smother it, the ball hit a clump of mud in the goalmouth and bobbled over his hands into the net.

'What a wally!' Danny hooted. 'Alex here could have walked over and picked that one up.'

I pulled a face at him but, I must admit, I reckon I could have. So could Tom if he'd been doing his job properly.

That's the annoying thing. It's not as if they're entirely useless, despite what I've said so far. They can both make decent stops at times and Danny's got a wicked kick on him too. He can really welly the ball away at goal kicks and that.

Anyway, we finished up losing 5–0, which dumped us on the bottom of the table with only two games left to play. But you can see what we've been up against this season. Danny and Tom together just bring out the worst in each other, not bothering if they help wreck the team's chances so long as they can put one over on their rival.

I don't know why Stubbsy hasn't put a stop to it before now. He must have realized what's been going on between them all the time. And even when they knew we'd *got* to win one of these matches to avoid getting relegated, they still carried on trying to sabotage one another's efforts.

You'll hardly believe it, but last Wednesday lunchtime, a few hours before the game which Stubbsy reckoned gave us our best hope of survival, I caught Danny hiding Tom's goalie gloves down the back of the radiator in the cloakroom. He whirled round when he heard somebody behind him, afraid it might be Tom, but then relaxed when he saw it was only me.

'You say a word to anybody, Alex, and I'll thump you,' he warned.

'Charming,' I said, knowing he wouldn't dare as I'd go straight to the dinner ladies to complain. 'I don't think what you're doing is very fair on Tom . . . nor on the team.'

'Who cares?' he chuckled. 'The grass's wet today and he won't be able to grip the ball properly without his gloves.'

'Doubt whether anybody will notice the difference,' I said, but Danny didn't appreciate my little jibe.

'Just shut it, you. What do you know about goalkeeping? Tom'll panic when he can't find his precious gloves and have to come and beg to borrow mine.'

'And I don't suppose you'll let him of course.'

'You bet I won't. I love to see him squirm.'

I gave Danny one of my hard stares. 'You wouldn't like it if he did something like that to you.'

'I make sure he doesn't get the chance. I don't leave important things like my goalie gloves just lying around anywhere.'

'Like in his bag,' I said, noticing Tom's unzipped sports bag on the bench.

'Yeah, well, same thing,' Danny grinned, a bit embarrassed, I felt, to have been caught actually going into somebody else's bag. 'I'm not nicking 'em or owt. I'll let him have 'em back again afterwards.'

'That's big of you,' I said sarcastically and waltzed out to find Tom. I mean, I wasn't taking sides or nothing, right, but I didn't see why everyone should suffer just 'cause of their petty squabbles.

I didn't tell tales on Danny, mind you. I'm not like that, but I made sure Tom knew where *somebody* had hidden his gloves as a joke. He didn't thank me of course – that's too much to expect – so all I got in reward were some dirty, suspicious looks from Danny when he saw Tom strutting about the cloakroom before the match waving his gloves in the air and looking well pleased with himself.

I soon found out why too. It wasn't just 'cause of the gloves. Suddenly there was a great shriek of rage from Danny that his boots had gone missing. I didn't need three guesses who was responsible, but Danny obviously must have had a couple, the way he swung round towards me straightaway.

He was dead mad, I'm not kidding. He probably thought I was getting my own back or something for the gloves nonsense till he saw Tom laughing his head off. I slunk away shaking mine, wondering why I bothered to interfere in the first place. You can't win either way.

The team certainly didn't. Nobody had any spare boots to fit Danny's big feet and he had to play in his white plimmies. He didn't half make a mess of 'em when he came on as sub and he couldn't do any of his power kicks. Worse still, he kept sliding about everywhere without studs and that cost us at least two goals when he slipped over trying to change position quick.

Mind you, I don't suppose it really mattered by that stage anyway. Tom had already spoilt things for us in the first half, letting one shot trickle in through his legs and fumbling another over the line. Fat lot of use those gloves of his turned out to be!

We lost 5–3 sadly and we seemed to be doomed. Maybe we still are, I don't know, but if we can *somehow* win our last game today then we'll stay up. At least now, though, I can do something positive myself to try and help. That's why I'm rabbiting on like this, I guess. It's nerves. Pre-match nerves.

Yep, that's right. I've finally made the side. I've actually been picked to play my very first game for South Millington Primary School football team.

In goal!

I was stunned when Stubbsy told me 'cause I've never played there before in my life. But perhaps even he's got fed up with all Danny and Tom's antics at last, or just decided the team can't very well do much worse with somebody different in goal. Either way, he's taking a big risk choosing me. I'm certainly different.

'I know you won't let us down, Alex,' he said, probably hiding crossed fingers in his pockets. 'Just do your best, and we'll have no worries, I'm sure.'

I hope he's right but, I mean, this is no fairy tale, even if it does all seem like a dream come true for me at the moment. I'd love to play a blinder and keep a clean sheet and all that, but who knows? Stubbsy's going to look a proper fool if things go wrong and I prove to be a disaster.

And if I was totally gobsmacked, imagine the shock Danny and Tom had when the teacher broke the news to them yesterday. I know – I was standing there right next to him when he did.

'Listen, lads,' Stubbsy began, 'I'm afraid I've had a change of mind about who's in goal for this final match . . .'

I was a bit sorry in a strange sort of way for them both when they heard. They must have felt terrible with it being me, of all people, taking their place. Like being slapped round the face with a long sweaty sock.

He even told them to stay away from the game so they couldn't come up behind the goal and start any of their funny business to distract me. Banning as well as dropping them was really rubbing their noses in it, but Stubbsy obviously meant to get his message across.

And he succeeded. I must have them worried. Last night they were seen actually practising together on the park, all pally again suddenly, trying to help each other improve.

It's never too late for miracles perhaps. But they've had their chance and now it's mine. Whatever happens today, I'm going to make them have

to work hard if they want to get back in the team next season.

Serves them right. I don't think they could somehow quite believe it at first, though, probably reckoning old Stubbsy was having them on. But you should have seen their poor little faces when they gradually realized he wasn't.

'You've picked Alex . . .?' Danny choked. 'To play in goal . . . instead of us . . .?'

'But . . . but . . . you can't do that . . .' Tom stammered. 'I mean, Alex is a . . .'

Stubbsy interrupted quickly. 'I'm fully aware what Alexandra is, thank you. That doesn't matter as far as I'm concerned. I watched her in action the other day, playing netball for the school, and her handling of the ball was excellent. I think she'll make a fine goalie.'

That certainly shut them up, yet the more I think about it too, I don't see why not. OK, so it might all mean I must be a touch crazy myself, like my dad says, but what's wrong with having a girl in goal?

I reckon this smart yellow jersey fits me real well! Wish me luck . . .

DAN

by Michelle Magorian

His dad had arranged to meet them near the ticket office at the Leisure Centre, but it was all too obvious when he and his mother had stared at the electronic doors for a quarter of an hour that his dad had been delayed.

'Nothing changes, does it?' his mother remarked at last.

'I expect he's been held up in the traffic,' Daniel protested. 'Saturday's always a bad day on the roads.'

'Every day's a bad day where your dad's concerned.'

'Please, Mum . . .' he began.

'I'll give him a call.'

'Don't start on him. He won't come if you do.'

'Don't worry,' she said, gritting her teeth. 'I'll be as nice as pie.'

Daniel sat on the steps next to the weighing machine and watched her at the payphone. A couple of years ago he wouldn't have believed that a slim-line version of her would be standing in a Leisure Centre, looking quite at home in a blue tracksuit and trainers. She had once been so overweight she had worn nothing but voluminous tent-like dresses. And because she had always been so miserable then, Daniel used to call her the Moaning Marquee. That was before she and his dad separated and divorced. Now he resented her looking so fit.

'Hello Mike! It's Julie.'

Daniel raised his eyes. His dad didn't need to be told her name.

'Daniel's waiting for you at the Leisure Centre with his swimming gear,' she said with artificial brightness. There was a pause. 'You can always wear dark underpants. No-one'll tell the difference.' She was now smiling so hard it looked like a grimace. 'He's been doing a lot of practice. I think he's hoping to get into a swimming team at Royston . . .' The smile faded. 'I didn't choose Royston. He did.' Another pause. 'No, I don't think it was because Royston doesn't have . . .' His mother had now gone red. 'Mike, not many comprehensives *do* rugby!'

Daniel sank his head into his hands. 'Mum, please,' he begged.

Back came the artificial smile.

'Anyway,' she added gaily. 'I still think you'll be impressed. He has a really good style now . . . OK, I'll tell him . . . Yes, well you'd better answer it then. Bye.'

She came over and leaned on the handrail.

'He says he'll be here in five minutes, but if there really was someone at the door I'd make that ten.'

Daniel nodded. He knew he should be pleased, but instead he felt as though a cement mixer was sitting on his chest.

'You know him, love,' she added softly.

Daniel looked hurriedly away. His eyes had begun to sting and he didn't want her to see.

'You go on home, Mum,' he said. 'I'll be all right.'

'I don't like to leave you here on your own.'

'I won't be alone for very long, will I?'

There was a pause.

'No,' she said quietly.

Because Daniel worshipped his father, his mother had agreed to let him stay with him every weekend, even though some judge had said every three weeks. His dad had his own flat now, so there was a room for Daniel to sleep in.

'I can easily wait,' she said.

'I don't want you to wait!' he snapped.

'OK. OK.'

She put down the rolled-up sleeping bag she was carrying by his feet.

'Take it away. You're embarrassing me.'

'You want somewhere to sleep tonight, don't you?'

'Look, I know he probably won't have had time to make my bed,' Daniel said wearily. 'I told you I don't mind making it myself.'

'That's if you can find it. You know what a slob . . . '

'He is not!' exploded Daniel. 'Just because he's not as tidy as you are . . .'

There was a moment's silence.

'I'll see you tomorrow night then,' she said, kissing the top of his head.

'Yeah,' he grunted.

'If you change your mind about having a go at rowing in the morning, give me a buzz and I'll give you a lift to the boathouse.'

'I won't change my mind.'

She hesitated for a moment, picked up the sleeping bag, and then turned quickly on her heel.

Daniel watched the electronic doors slide open for her. He kept his eyes on her as she walked through the car park, hoping she wouldn't look back. He had made up his mind that, if his father hadn't turned up in ten minutes, he would go to the pool on his own.

He swam thirty lengths. He kidded himself that his dad would have been impressed, even though he knew that only one sport existed for his father.

Before going into the pool, he had undressed with painstaking slowness, expecting him to burst through the door at any moment. Later, when he was swimming, he kept checking to see if he was coming out of the changing rooms. Even as he dried and dressed himself, he half expected to have to put on his wet trunks again and go back in the pool with him. But of course he never came. Daniel stood in the foyer watching people entering and leaving in groups and pairs, chatting and laughing, and he felt a loneliness so overwhelming it physically hurt.

He stared at the payphone, but he couldn't bring himself to dial his father's number in case he answered.

Then he had an idea.

He ran swiftly over to the ticket office. A young woman with long glossy hair smiled down at him.

'Had a good swim?' she asked cheerily.

'Yeah.' And he smiled back. Her happiness was infectious. 'How did you guess?'

'Your hair's wet. Do you want to use one of the courts or the athletics track now?'

'No. I was just wondering if you'd seen a big man come in here in the last half hour.'

'With a beer belly?'

'Yeah. That's him.'

'He went up to the canteen.' She gave him the directions.

He raced up the stairs, half stumbling with excitement, weaving in and out of a group of men and women with squash rackets who were coming down.

He burst through the swing doors on the landing and across a long stretch of floor, down a corridor and past the bar. The canteen doors were about ten metres away. He slowed down, his heart beating, slung his bag over his shoulder and strolled towards the door, grinning.

The young woman was right. There was a big man sitting in the canteen, but it wasn't his dad.

Daniel gazed at him in disbelief. The man looked up. Daniel quickly made for the counter. He would have to buy himself something now. It would look daft if he walked in and out.

'Excuse me!'

A loud voice made him swing round. A tall lean man, dressed in a white singlet, long slim-fitting white trousers which hooked over the feet and white canvas shoes which looked like a cross between plimsolls and ballet shoes, was standing at the door.

'I only have three people in my trampoline group,' he announced. 'Seems everyone is away on holiday. I need a fourth person to cover one side otherwise I'll have to cancel and send the others home. Any chance of a volunteer?'

'Not me, mate,' boomed the tank he'd wished was his dad.

The man laughed. 'That's all right, I was hoping for someone younger.'

Daniel wasn't quite sure what it was that made him raise his arm. Maybe it was the silence which made him feel awkward. But he hardly had any time to regret it because the beam on the man's face made him feel he had handed him the Crown Jewels.

'Great!' he said.

Daniel ambled shyly towards him.

'I really appreciate you giving us your time,' said the man as they squeezed through the doorway together.

It was while they were striding down the long open space towards the swing doors that the man put his hand on Daniel's shoulder. Normally Daniel would have been acutely embarrassed, but there was something in the man's manner which made him feel relaxed. 'My name's Stewart,' he said. 'What's yours?'

Daniel was about to say 'Titch'. It was what everyone called him, including the teachers, at his junior school. Did. He wouldn't be seeing them again. He would be starting at the Royston Road comprehensive in a month. .

'Dan,' he said suddenly. It was like putting on a new identity. It made him sound strong, straightforward.

The three trampolinists were a tall gangly West Indian girl called Kathryn, a stocky muscular

24

fourteen-year-old called Markos, who looked Greek, and a petite fair-haired girl called Cherry. Kathryn, who had what Dan called a 'la-di-da' accent, hunched herself over as if trying to appear smaller, Cherry giggled a lot and Markos stared at Stewart all the time frowning with concentration. Daniel immediately sensed an undercurrent of excitement.

Cherry was the first to get on to the trampoline.

'Cherry,' said Stewart, 'I know you have beautiful hair, but I told you, if you wear it loose like that you'll blind yourself. Anyone got an elastic band?'

Cherry stood in her neat pink shorts and matching T-shirt and stared at him in dismay. Even when she was horrified she still looked pretty, thought Daniel.

Stewart climbed up on to the trampoline and tied her hair back with the lace of a trainer. Mortified, she flung her hands over her face.

'I look awful,' she protested.

'You look lovely,' said Stewart, sliding neatly off the trampoline. 'And you know it.'

She giggled and began jumping up and down.

To Daniel's surprise she was completely graceless. As she soared in the air, her legs and arms flew in all directions. Even Daniel could see she was jumping too fast.

'Start from scratch,' said Stewart. 'Feet apart. Arms slightly raised beside you. Now bend your knees, push those heels into the webbing and jump. Bring your legs together and point your toes.'

She flung herself up but every time she landed it was in a different place. Now Daniel realized why they needed all sides covered.

'Remember,' Stewart shouted, 'when you see her coming towards you, don't step back. Step forward and push her back towards the centre.'

Tracking her, as she flew like a floppy rag doll in all directions, took all of Daniel's concentration. Eventually she managed to jump with her knees tucked up and later with her legs apart in a straddle. But as soon as she hit the trampoline she fell over.

'Good try, Cherry, but remember when you land, it's feet apart and bend your knees quickly.'

Flushed with tiredness, she nodded, sat on the edge and slid ungainly to the ground.

It was Markos' turn next.

'Wow!' Dan whispered, as Markos thumped his feet firmly into the canvas and soared into the air. He threw his legs well apart in a straddle, touching his toes. As soon as his feet hit the canvas he was up into a pike, legs drawn in front of him together, and touching his toes. Then to Dan's amazement he slammed his feet back into the canvas, and hardly had he left it than he drove his elbows down beside him and did a somersault, landing with precision on his feet.

Dan was about to yell out 'fantastic', when Stewart interrupted.

'Not bad, Markos. You have a good driving spin there, but it's a gymnastic somersault, not a trampoline one.'

He was criticizing him! Daniel was gobsmacked. He had just done a somersault and the man was criticizing him!

'Wally!' whispered Daniel crossly.

But Markos was standing with his powerful hands on his hips, nodding.

'I know,' he said. 'I'm so used to doing somersaults on a mat I go into the old shoulders-down routine automatically.'

'What did he do wrong?' asked Daniel. 'It looked great to me.'

'When you do a somersault on the floor you need to drive your shoulders down really hard, whereas a lot of the things we do on the trampoline are based on hip movements, not shoulders. Here, I'll show you.'

Markos slipped off the trampoline to cover for Stewart.

'Now my hips will take me halfway through the somersault. Height first, hips back, then tuck. That's why we practise the tuck jump. It's good preparation for a somersault.'

Dan watched Stewart glide up into the air. At the height of his third jump, he jerked his hips back and tucked, and Dan could see what he meant. His somersault was nowhere near the canvas. He span at the height of the jump and then gracefully unfolded out of it, his body unbending, hips forward like a curved bow.

'Have another try,' he said swinging himself off the trampoline.

Markos bounced back on to the canvas.

'And let's see if you can straighten your knees and point your toes,' he added.

'I'm pointing them as hard as I can!'

'I know,' said Stewart smiling, 'and it shows. You have far more stretch than you had two months ago. We'll have those legs straight yet. Now wait till I tell you to turn.'

Markos began to thump his feet into the canvas again, soaring up again, a compact square of muscle, neat, feet together but knees still bent.

'Now!' yelled Stewart.

Markos bent his arms and whipped them down. He span and descended speedily in Daniel's direction.

Daniel gritted his teeth and flung his arms out in front of him. Immediately Kathryn was by his side and in a second they had pushed Markos back to the centre.

Daniel watched mesmerized as Markos repeatedly grew worse and worse. So much for trampoline somersaults, he thought, glaring at Stewart.

'You're trying too hard,' said Stewart. 'You're putting enough energy in for a double, if not a triple somersault. Remember, hips, a quick tuck and unfold. Try counting "one".'

Markos nodded.

Daniel could see the intensity of Markos' concentration as he jumped powerfully down into the trampoline. He was convinced Stewart had got it all wrong. Perhaps he was jealous of Markos. But to Daniel's amazement, Markos showed respect for Stewart.

Markos was still jumping, still not attempting the somersault. What is he waiting for? thought Daniel, feeling tense with excitement. Then as Markos reached the top of the next jump, Daniel watched his hips jerk back and at the last moment he snapped in his knees, let them go instantly and arched his body as he descended. As his feet touched the canvas he bent his knees sharply and he was as solid as a rock.

To Daniel's surprise he found himself clapping along with Cherry and Kathryn.

'I got it!' Markos yelled.

'How did it feel?' asked Stewart.

'Weird. It really felt as if I wasn't trying hard enough. It's such a quick tuck!'

Stewart nodded. 'Like to try a swivel hips?'

Markos gave a loud groan and collapsed on to the canvas. 'Is this my reward?'

'Come on,' said Stewart. 'You conquered the single somersault.'

The swivel hips consisted of jumping into a sitting position called a seat drop, rising, doing half a turn, sitting on the other side and bouncing back on to the feet.

Markos managed to do the 'seat drop' but instead of swivelling he tucked up his knees and kept trying to go sideways into the second seat drop.

'Sorry, but it's just not going in,' said Markos sitting on the canvas.

'Let's get back to basics,' suggested Stewart. 'Do a seat drop into a front drop. That will get you used to swinging your legs underneath you.'

Markos scrambled back up to his feet. He was about to begin thumping into the canvas when Stewart stopped him.

'Do it from standing. You don't need so much height.'

Markos stood with his legs apart, threw himself into a seat drop and as he rose into the air from it, he drew his legs back underneath him, landed full length on to his front and back on to his feet.

'There, not so bad was it?' exclaimed Stewart. 'Now remember the feeling of your legs swinging underneath you, but keep straight and add a half turn into a seat drop the other side.'

Markos tried but instead of adding the half turn he kept bringing his knees up into a tuck and falling over.

After a few more turns, Stewart suggested he take a break and have another crack at it later.

It was Kathryn's turn next. As she hauled her long lean limbs clumsily on to the trampoline, she gave the appearance of a dark brown spider.

She was wearing tight-fitting black Bermuda shorts which reminded Daniel of his mother's rowing shorts, and a brightly coloured vest in orange and black. To Daniel's amazement, as soon as she began jumping, she seemed to elongate out like a stretched rubber band.

Taking her time, her legs straight and pointed, she soared upwards like an arrow. She waited until she was at the height of her jump before she did a straddle or a pike jump and it was breathtakingly beautiful to watch.

She then jumped into a seat drop, her feet so pointed, her legs so straight you could have put a ruler across them. As she rose back into the air she drew her legs underneath her, twisted as though twisting a hoola hoop round her waist and landed in a seat drop on the other side.

Daniel clapped and then suddenly felt self-conscious. Stewart was smiling at him.

'Yes,' he agreed. 'That's how a swivel hips should look.'

Daniel glanced over at Cherry and Markos to see if they were jealous but they were too absorbed in watching her. There was a really good feeling of • support around the trampoline. So much so that he suddenly wanted to be up there jumping too. Meanwhile he watched Kathryn soaring gracefully and powerfully to a tremendous height. Suddenly she did a single somersault, unfolded out of it and to Daniel's horror appeared to be falling on her way down. Instead she landed in a front drop, tucked up round to another front drop on the other side and was back on to her feet again.

Daniel was so absorbed in watching her, that Stewart had to speak several times to him before his question finally penetrated.

'Me?' he exclaimed. 'Up there?'

'If you want.'

He looked at the others. 'Won't they mind?'

But he could see by their shaking heads that they didn't.

'You won't be doing somersaults today though.'

Daniel laughed, and it shook him by its unfamiliarity. It was then that he realized he hadn't laughed for a very long time. He didn't even get uptight when he couldn't get on to the trampoline. Markos came round and cupped his hands into a step for him. And Daniel collapsed laughing again as he sprawled spread-eagled on to the canvas.

'When you've recovered,' said Stewart, 'start by just jumping on the canvas. Get used to the feel of it. It's springier than some trampolines, being webbed, and you'd better do it in your socks.'

Daniel threw his trainers on to the floor, bent his knees and dug his heels into the canvas.

'You're quick,' said Stewart, surprised. 'Have you done anything like this before?'

'No,' said Daniel.

'Gymnastics?'

'No.'

'You can point your feet as well as Kathryn.'

Daniel could feel himself beginning to blush. He prayed he wouldn't be asked any more questions. 'I've dived a bit,' he said hurriedly.

'Like to have a go at the swivel hips?' Stewart asked.

'Yeah!'

The others laughed at his eagerness.

'Now remember, swing your legs underneath you as you rise.'

Daniel nodded.

He stood with his legs apart, feet parallel on the webbed canvas and pushed off into a seat drop. Then with all the strength he could muster he swung his legs underneath him.

'Turn!' yelled Stewart.

The next thing he knew he was facing the other side but on his back. He was just about to curse when to his surprise he heard the others clapping.

'That's a great start!' said Stewart.

'Really?' said Daniel, hauling himself up to his feet.

'Again?' asked Stewart.

Daniel grinned. He stood with his feet apart again, raised his arms and pushed himself up into the air.

After they had folded the trampoline and wheeled it back against one of the walls in the gym, Markos and Cherry went off into a corner and chatted. One of Daniel's trainers had landed by a crimson tracksuit. He found that he and Kathryn were heading in the same direction.

As he pulled on his shoes, he watched her hauling on the tracksuit trousers out of the corner of his eye and he suddenly felt shy.

'You're good,' he blurted out.

She looked down at him and beamed. 'Thanks.'

She sat beside him and pulled on her shoes.

'You don't do yoga by any chance?' he added casually.

'No.' She looked hesitant for a moment. 'If I tell you something will you promise to keep quiet about it?'

'Yeah. Course.'

'I do ballet,' she whispered.

'What's wrong with that?' he asked surprised.

'Look at the height of me. I'm only eleven and I'm still growing. My mother's convinced I'll be nearly two metres by the time I've finished. Can you imagine what people would think of a beanpole like me doing ballet! They'd laugh their heads off.'

'Is that why you hunch yourself over?'

'Do I?'

He nodded. 'Except when you're on the trampoline and then you look really graceful.'

She gave a bashful smile.

'Actually,' he said slowly, 'I have a secret to confess too.'

'You do ballet too?'

'Much worse. My dad calls me and Mum cranky. He says we'll be turning vegetarian next.'

'Why?'

'Because we . . .' he paused. 'Are you ready for this?'

'Yes,' she said impatiently. 'Go on.'

'We do yoga.'

'Oh. So that's why you thought I did it.'

'Yes. Don't tell anyone. I'm only supposed to do it in secret at my mum's. My dad hates it. He says if I ever do it in public or in front of any of his rugby-loving friends, he'll pretend he doesn't know me.'

'I'm afraid I don't know much about yoga.'

'I'll show you a lotus position.'

He gave a quick look round but the hall was empty. He sat cross legged and folded his feet over the opposite thighs.

'Doesn't that hurt?' she gasped.

'No. You have to work up to it though.'

'But how did you start it if your dad . . .'

'I didn't. My mum started doing it first, three years ago, for her nerves.'

'Did it work?'

'Yes. She stopped moaning and started getting more confident. Only snag was she got so confident she asked my dad for a divorce, and I took it up for *my* nerves!'

Kathryn laughed. She grabbed her tracksuit top. 'I'm going upstairs for a snack. Want to come?'

Daniel hesitated for a moment. His dad might worry if he was late. He smiled. So what! Let him have a taste of his own medicine. 'Yeah,' he said. 'Why not?'

His father's flat was only five flights of stairs up, but to his annoyance, he had found himself leaping up the stairs two at a time, instead of walking. He stopped for a moment to catch his breath and wipe the sweat from his face. He didn't want to look exhausted when he made his entrance.

As soon as he reached the fifth-floor landing he noticed that the door was ajar. He hesitated, alarmed. Perhaps there had been a break-in. Perhaps his father was lying in a pool of blood, bound and gagged on the sitting room floor. That would explain why he hadn't arrived at the Leisure Centre.

Cautiously he sidled towards the door and pushed it open.

Scattered across the tiny hallway were suitcases, newspapers and chairs. The place had been ransacked. He felt sick. 'Dad,' he called out shakily.

There was no answer. From behind the closed sitting room door he heard the sounds of a television.

'Dad,' he began again.

A loud yell came from behind the door. 'Stop him you silly . . .' It was him.

'Oh no,' yelled a second voice.

Furious, Daniel threw open the sitting room door with such ferocity that the door knob hit the wall.

His father was sitting on the settee staring at the box. Another man Daniel didn't know was sitting in the nearby armchair. By their feet was a row of empty beer cans.

'Hi, Titch,' said his father cheerfully over his shoulder. 'Good to see you!'

Daniel strode angrily across the room and stood in front of the screen.

'Hey, Titch, stop larking about,' protested his father.

'Dad, you were supposed to meet me at the Leisure Centre. Remember?'

'Sorry mate, I completely forgot Trev was coming round. I left a message to say forget about the swimming and come round and watch this.'

Daniel turned. 'Rugby? In the summer!' he exclaimed. 'Wait a minute. You've seen this match before.'

'I know. It's so fantastic. You'll learn a lot from these players. Trev brought it round on his video. Good of him, wasn't it?'

Daniel glanced briefly at the man in the armchair. The man gave him a cheery wave. With their beer bellies, he and his dad looked like Tweedledee and Tweedledum.

'You could have watched this later,' Daniel said pointedly.

'Trev was only here for the afternoon. I knew you'd understand.'

'I don't, Dad.'

'Hey, you're not upset, are you?'

'I'm angry, Dad.'

'Titch,' he said quietly. 'We have a guest.'

'My name is Dan. I'm not going to answer to Titch any more.'

'All right, your name is not Titch. Look, I'm sorry. Now if you don't mind,' he indicated the set.

'Did your guest know you were supposed to meet me?'

'Yes, but I told him you'd understand when you got the message.'

'I didn't get the message.'

'That's not my fault, is it? Why didn't you phone?'

'Because . . .' he felt lost for words. 'You still should have come!'

'Come on, Titch . . .'

With that Daniel turned off the set.

A flush of colour swept across his father's face. 'You've gone too far,' he began.

'I want an apology.'

'You've had it. How many more times do I have to say I'm sorry?'

Daniel switched on the set and stormed out of the room. He heard his father rewind the video. 'Kids!' he heard him mutter to his friend. 'I left a message. What more could I do?'

Daniel opened the kitchen door. Seven days ago he had scrubbed and washed the kitchen and helped his dad move in. He had been so angry with his mother for not helping out that they had had a major quarrel. When finally he had yelled 'But why not?' she had just answered quietly, 'Because it's just a waste of time.'

Now tins of every variety surrounded the over-flowing rubbish bin which was leaning precariously against the sink unit. Stacked high in the washing-up bowl and on the draining board was a week's worth of unwashed crockery.

He stared stunned at the filthy floor. It wasn't just the disbelief that his father could live like this, he just couldn't work out how mud could reach a fifth-floor flat.

He backed into the corridor and climbed over the suitcases and newspapers towards his bedroom.

The door was stuck. He leaned against it, thrust his arm round and grabbed a holdall, pushing it and a towel to one side. The door fell open.

It was only too obvious that his father had been using the room as a dumping ground.

'It's only temporary,' he said, mimicking his father's jovial voice. But then any mess he made always was 'only temporary'.

His dad was the procrastinator of all time. He

could have won an Oscar for it. He procrastinated so much that Daniel sometimes wondered how he ever managed to get born.

For a moment he stood in the debris, too numbed with disappointment and hurt to move. There was no sign of his bed. Like the floor it was submerged under a mountain of shoes, magazines, boxes, tools and bulging bin-liners.

It was all over. He had been defeated. There was no way his parents would ever get back together again now. His mother wouldn't want to give up her rowing and training sessions to restart cleaning up after his dad. And however much Daniel tried to help him, his dad would never change. In fact he had grown worse.

As he gazed at the mess, feeling thoroughly depressed, he was suddenly conscious of a sense of relief.

'That's it!' he muttered angrily. 'From now on I'll please myself. They'll just have to sort out their own problems.' And with that he picked up two bin bags and hurled them determinedly off the bed.

Later, in the kitchen, while the kettle was boiling, Daniel wiped some tomato sauce from the telephone receiver and dialled. His mother must have been waiting for him. The phone was picked up instantly.

'Mum, I've changed my mind about tomorrow. I'd like to have a crack at the rowing.'

There was silence.

'Mum?'

'He didn't turn up, did he?' she said at last.

'No.'

He heard her sigh. 'I'm sorry, love.'

'It's OK, I had a fantastic time. I went on a trampoline.'

'On your own?'

'No. There was a coach there. He said I'm good.'

'Great!'

'And I met this girl there called Kathryn. We went to the canteen afterwards and it turns out she's starting at Royston Road next term too.'

'Every cloud has a silver lining, eh?'

'Sort of.'

'Have you told Dad?'

'No. He's busy.'

'Watching *Grandstand*?'

'No. Rugby. It's a video.'

'Oh.' There was a brief pause. 'I'll pick you up about nine thirty then.'

'Do you mind if I pop round for breakfast?'

'No. I'll come round about eight then, shall I?'

'No. I can walk.'

'Are you sure?'

'Mum, it's only three streets away.'

'Do you want me to drop you at Dad's after the rowing?'

'I'll see how I feel.'

'Don't take it to heart. Your dad doesn't mean to hurt you.'

'I know. Mum?'

'Yes.'

'There's something I want to say.'

'Yes?'

'It's about rugby.'

'Oh.'

'No, listen.' He took a deep breath. 'I want you to know that if I ever do decide to play rugby, it won't be because I'm trying to please Dad and it won't be because you don't like macho games and I'm trying to get up your nose. It'll be because I want to do it. OK?'

'Fine. As long as you clean your muddy boots and wash your kit.'

He laughed. That was typical of his mother now.

'*Do* you want to play rugby?' she asked hesitantly.

'Not now. But I might later. Who knows?' He paused. 'There's something else, too. Don't introduce me as Titch tomorrow, will you? I don't want to be called that any more.'

'I never do anyway.'

With a surprise he realized it was true. He had spent so much time trying to get his father's attention that he had hardly noticed what his mother said or did.

'Why don't you, Mum?'

'You don't seem small to me.'

'But I am.'

'Well, if I got out a tape measure. Yes. Probably. But you're so packed with energy, you've always seemed on the big side to me.'

He smiled. 'Thanks, Mum.'

He made three mugs of tea, took them into the sitting room and handed one to Trev.

'Thanks, Dan,' he said.

He gave a mug to his father.

'All right now?' asked his dad.

Daniel nodded and sat beside him on the settee.

His father raised his mug. 'Cheers, then.'

'Cheers,' said Daniel, and he sat back, drew up his legs and watched rugby league in the lotus position.

DOUBLE-BOOKED

By Judith Hemington

Sanjay came to the point on his way home where he had to make a decision. Long way round or short-cut? Only it wasn't as straightforward as that. The short-cut involved passing the bus stop, and that was a problem, because hanging around the bus stop with nothing better to do than to make his life a misery would be a bunch of older boys and a couple of girls: they regarded that bus stop as their patch.

He took a deep breath and went for the short-cut – partly because he didn't like to think that a gang of thugs could rule his life; and partly because he was feeling particularly happy and so was in a mood to take a chance.

If only his family still lived in the old house things would have been much simpler, he thought. There, he had friends to go home with and to play cricket with after school. On this new estate they were the only Asian family. Neighbours were polite, but . . .

He tensed as the bus stop came in view. They were there. Sanjay was no coward, but he knew he wouldn't stand a chance with that lot, and although stronger than he looked, he wasn't as tall as he would have liked.

Passing a crowd of hostile boys is rather like passing through a field of bulls. You can feel them staring at you, and you get a prickly feeling at the back of the neck, and you don't know whether to stare them out and show you're not scared, or to keep your eyes on the ground and pretend you haven't noticed them. Neither of these worked very well, in Sanjay's experience.

He crossed to the other side. The road trembled, and two big buses lumbered up and stopped, cutting Sanjay off from the gang's immediate line of vision. By the time they had finished annoying the people getting off the bus, Sanjay was well past. It was his lucky day. First that exciting notice in the school: now, saved by a couple of buses!

He walked swiftly, but did not run, and then with relief he turned into his road, and breathed in the smell of yellow blossom from the garden on the corner. His uncle's car was outside his house, he noted. He enjoyed a visit from him. It also meant that his parents would be home early and there would be something special for supper.

Delicious spicy smells wafted out as he opened the door. Just what he needed.

'School all right? No trouble?' There was just a slightly anxious look there as his mother asked him.

'No – no trouble. School was OK.' He wouldn't tell her even if there was trouble. No point.

His uncle twisted his head round stiffly in his chair. 'You doing well at school?' he asked. Sanjay dipped his large, brown eyes. He hated answering questions like that.

'He does very well,' his father said, his voice solemn and full of pride.

'They're going to start a cricket team at school,' Sanjay said – to change the subject, and also because if he didn't tell someone soon this important news he knew he'd burst. 'There's a new teacher, and he's keen so . . .'

'A cricket team, are they? So will they choose you?' his uncle asked in his slow, wondering voice.

Sanjay shrugged. 'I'm going to try for it.'

'So you want to be like your cousin Ranjeet? You know, he went for trials at Leicester. Natural sportsman, they said. He's waiting to hear, you know.'

Of course Sanjay knew. Every night since his other uncle had phoned, brimming over with the news, Sanjay had been thinking about it – imagining what it would be like: picturing himself in Ranjeet's place clumping on to the pitch with his pads, hitting balls over boundaries with elegant strokes.

'We don't want Sanjay getting swept away with too much of this cricket idea. He mustn't forget his studies,' his father said.

Sanjay felt angry inside. Always his studies! His studies! And then at school, because he had always done the work, the boys would make fun of him, call him a swot. You couldn't win. Sometimes he felt like a clove of garlic crushed in a garlic press, parents and school on either side.

'They'll never let you into a team, man! You've only played with kids on the street!' Typical Rama. Always putting him down – just because he, Rama, was three years older. The really annoying thing was that he would always be three years older.

Sanjay decided not to bother to start an argument, not with his uncle there. He'd show Rama! He'd get into that team and just show him! For a few seconds he felt hot and excited and confident, and then all the certainty suddenly melted away.

'Sanjay, can you tell me the greatest enemy of soldiers in the First World War?'

Sanjay's stomach did an anxious leap, and he tugged his eyes and thoughts away from the blue sky beckoning from beyond the window. Today all he could think of was the first session of cricket 'for anyone who was interested', after school.

'Mud, they thought was the enemy, Miss Tilsen,' he said, his nervousness speeding up the words.

'What did you say?'

Sanjay froze. He could feel the eyes of the rest of the class fixed on him, beady eyes, unfriendly eyes, wanting him to fail. Perhaps she'd asked something totally different. 'Mud?' he said again.

'Yes, that's it. You spoke too fast first time.'

Sanjay heard the boy behind mimicking his accent, and he wished he could be a million miles away from the classroom and the people in it.

But soon it would be over, and then . . . As he gathered his books together at the end of the lesson he felt something inside him thumping, pounding. Perhaps he'd be no good: since they'd moved house he hadn't had much practice. His mother was always urging him to go out to join the boys playing cricket on the green, but she didn't understand.

You could only go and hover near a game if you knew someone would draw you in. No-one there would ease him into the game. They weren't bullies – not like some of the people at the school – but they just wouldn't bother. Probably wouldn't himself if it was the other way around.

Jason Stevens and Mickey O'Halloran were walking down the corridor ahead of him. They were probably going where he was going. Shame about that. Mickey was OK. He had carrot-red hair and a big grin. Jason was something else. His brother did body-building and walked like a gorilla, and Jason copied his brother's way of walking. He looked more like an American foot-baller, even without the shoulder pads, than a cricket player, Sanjay thought. Jason had a head like a huge bullet; small, sullen eyes and a thin, mean mouth.

Jason happened to glance over his shoulder and saw Sanjay behind. He nudged Mickey, who looked around too. Mickey said something, and they both laughed – a threatening laugh, it was. That was the trouble with people like Jason: their meanness was catching.

Sanjay's neck tensed. His breathing quickened, and he wished he didn't have to go to the changing rooms with those two. They were bound to try something – push him in the showers, grab his shorts and throw them some place out of reach. Oh well, there was nothing for it . . .

And then the idea popped into his mind that he could perhaps change in the boys' toilets on the other side of the school. He glanced at his watch. Five minutes. He could do it. Just as Jason turned out of sight down the steps, Sanjay darted back down the corridor and past the hall and down the steps. Breathless he flung himself into the boys' toilets, which smelt as horrible as they always did, and ripped off his clothes. Then he steamed out across the yard and over to the part of the field where a little crowd was gathered. In fact it was quite a large crowd: something to do with England actually doing well in the Test against Australia that year. Sanjay felt proud that he had been keen on cricket even *before* this. It was a family tradition.

'How d'you get here?' Jason asked, poking San-jay in the ribs to make his point, his little eyes bulging with surprise.

Sanjay reckoned it was none of Jason's business, but decided he needed a few more kilos of muscle on his body, and about thirty centimetres more in height before he'd be in a position to mention this to Jason, so he said: 'Had to run and get something I left behind.'

'You was quick,' Jason said.

This was the longest conversation Sanjay had ever had with Jason, and he didn't fancy carrying it on much longer, so he was relieved when Mr Philips then called: 'Right, lads, we'd better get started. There are a couple of things I want to say before we get stuck in. One, I want everyone in the team or possibly in the team to give their one hundred per cent to it. Dedication's the name of the game. OK? You're either in and giving your all, or you're out. See? Two, my word's law. No messing about. Cricket balls can be pretty dangerous weapons if someone's being careless, and I don't want to have to explain to anyone's grieving mum that her little Johnny has just snuffed it because he was thinking of something else when a cricket ball hit him between the eyes. Right? OK, let's go. We'll set up two games, so nobody's hanging around for too long with nothing to do.'

Jason was one of the first four in to bat. Funny how some people always seem to get what they want, Sanjay thought. He himself was stuck way out as a fielder. Not many balls came his way, but one sped really fast out towards the boundary. He pounded after it and hurled it back.

'Nice bit of fielding there!' Mr Philips called, and Sanjay glowed inside. A little later Mr Philips came over and said: 'You've got a good throw – we'll see how you do at a spot of bowling.'

Sanjay's hand was trembling so much that he felt sure he'd drop the ball before he had a chance to get it into the air.

Just occasionally in life the impossible happens. Not very often, but just every once in a while, coincidence strikes, magic seems to rule. This was such a moment, for the ball left Sanjay's hand, soared into the air, and with deadly aim seemed to melt through Jason's bat and strike the wicket at

the other side. Sanjay was surprised. Jason was surprised. Everyone was surprised. There were gasps. Mouths hung open. Jason was so taken aback that he forgot that he had to leave the crease, and was not too pleased when someone reminded him of this fact.

Dazed, Sanjay prepared to launch his second ball. Perhaps the magic would work twice. It didn't, of course, but that didn't matter. One triumph was enough for one day.

When the practice was over Mr Philips gathered everyone around and told them who he wanted to see at the next practice. Sanjay was one of the chosen. He was bursting to tell Rama, and raced home without even thinking of the gang that haunted the bus stop. Fortunately the gang was otherwise engaged elsewhere.

'I don't believe you!' Rama said when informed of the bowling triumph. 'You're just having me on, man!'

'Honestly, it's true!' Sanjay said.

'Well, if it is true, it's a fluke.'

'OK, so it's a fluke! So what? I'm in the team. He said I have a good throw.'

'It's not a team yet. You haven't got chosen to play in a proper match.'

'Nobody's got chosen to play in a proper match yet!'

From this moment cricket became Sanjay's passion. He had been *keen* on cricket before – but now . . . In his dreams he heard balls landing on cricket bats with a satisfying click, right where they should land; he saw blurred balls scudding towards boundaries; bails leaping off wickets; balls plopping into cupped hands. Whenever he could he would practise – only it's not easy to practise cricket on your own. He would try out his bowling action, do imaginary elegant batting strokes, persuade Rama to play. A game of cricket is a magnetic thing. Boys would trickle out of houses, eye them enviously, and Rama would draw them into the game. The new estate seemed a less unfriendly place after that.

At meal times, all Sanjay could think about was cricket scores, and how he would do at the next practice. Conversation of adults would babble meaninglessly over his head – talk of cousins and weddings and holidays. As soon as he could, he would ease himself away from the table so that he could get any homework done and be free to wheedle Rama out to practise a few strokes before the sun dipped out of the sky and the light died out of the day.

'I've been making some arrangements,' Mr Philips announced. 'We need something to work for, so I've been on the phone and I've got us some fixtures with local schools. We're nowhere near ready yet – so I want some hard work – but let's see what you can do! In the next couple of weeks I'll decide who's going to be in the team. I'll put up the list of fixtures on the noticeboard, so make sure you keep those Saturdays free.'

From then on they had three sessions a week after school. When Sanjay played badly he wanted to dig a hole in the ground and bury himself in it. Life just wasn't worth living. When he did well everything around him seemed to brighten up – even people seemed friendlier when he'd sent a ball whizzing into the distance, unstoppable, or had caught a ball he had never expected to catch.

There were twenty people who came regularly to cricket practice. Some would have to be disappointed. As the Saturday of the first match came closer you could feel the tension mounting.

'He'll put the list up Thursday morning, I expect,' someone said. Sanjay could think of nothing else.

'Sanjay, you're not listening to me!' his mother said. 'I'm putting your clothes for Saturday on the chair in your room. You mustn't touch them before then.' He smiled, still not really listening, and edged out of the door. That night he couldn't sleep.

Lists dangled tantalizingly before his eyes. Sometimes his name was on, sometimes it wasn't, and sometimes the writing in his dream was so blurred that he couldn't read whether his name was on or not. In the last practice he'd dropped an easy catch. He kept on waking up and re-living that experience, the ball slipping through his hands. Heartbreaking! Why in the last practice, of all times! There was also something else bothering him as he tossed and turned, but he wasn't sure what. Something someone had said.

At break he could tell by the scrum of people pushing and shoving near the board that the list was up. 'You're in, Mickey!' someone called.

'What about me? Am I there? I'd better be!' That was Jason's hoarse voice.

Sanjay hung back: it was pointless trying to push past that lot. And anyway, he probably wouldn't be in. Why choose someone who couldn't catch?

Just before the buzzer sounded for the end of break he darted in front of the list. The names seemed to dance about at first, but his name was there. They'd spelt it wrong, but who cared! Happiness shot up like a fountain inside him. He was going to enjoy telling Rama this.

At the end of the day, after the practice, he burst through the front door. 'Mum! Rama! I'm in the team for Saturday!' he yelled.

His mother came into the hall to greet him. 'Why are you shouting?' she asked.

'I'm in the team, I'm in the team to play Rushden School on Saturday!'

She didn't hug him; she didn't smile. Her eyes seemed to become bigger and rounder, and she said: 'But Sanjay, on Saturday you're going to Rupa's wedding in London.'

In an instant, the joy drained out of Sanjay's life. 'But I can't! I've just got to play! I'm on the list. Mr Philips would be mad if I didn't.' His eyes held hers. She had to relent. He hardly knew his cousin, Rupa. Surely he could stay behind. She wouldn't notice if he wasn't there amongst all the guests.

'You must come to the wedding, Sanjay. You must have known about it! We've been talking about it for weeks. Remember, I put your clothes out? Rupa would be offended if you didn't come. You know you have to come.'

Sanjay remembered all those boring conversations he hadn't really listened to. His body sagged. He knew there was no hope. He wasn't sure what was worse: the disappointment of not being able to play, or the dread of telling Mr Philips that he couldn't play.

At break next morning he steeled himself to

make his way to the staffroom. As he approached, he saw Mickey O'Halloran waiting outside the door. He didn't look too happy either.

'Watcha, Sanjay!' he said in a reasonably friendly way, and before Sanjay had time to reply a teacher and a blast of cigarette smoke came out of the staffroom.

'What can I do for you both?' he asked, in the slightly mocking tone teachers often adopt.

'I want to see Mr Philips,' Mickey said.

'I would like to see him too,' Sanjay said quickly.

'I think he may be busy just at the minute, but I'll let him know,' the teacher said.

'That means Philips will finish his fag first,' Mickey said as the door closed. 'What d'you want to see him for, anyway?'

'There's a wedding in my family on Saturday, so I won't be able to play. He's going to be angry, isn't he!'

'You bet he is – especially since I'm just about to tell him that I can't play because me dad dropped a brick on his foot and broke his toe, so he says I've got to help me uncle on the stall Saturday instead of him. Families! Who needs them!'

'Right, lads, what is it?' Mr Philips appeared at the door. His face didn't look too promising: it looked even less promising when Mickey had explained the problem. Before Mr Philips could reply to Mickey, Sanjay quickly slipped in his own difficulty with Saturday, and then waited for the storm to break.

'So this is what you mean by team spirit, is it? For Pete's sake, why didn't you tell me before, so I didn't put you in the team? It's Friday now. We play tomorrow. What d'you expect me to do? I told you to keep these Saturdays free.'

There was a short silence. He glanced at the two boys, who dipped their eyes and stared miserably at the floor. 'Well, you know what I said at the beginning, don't you! It's all or nothing. If you choose to spend your Saturdays earning a few bob down the market or dolling yourself up for weddings, that's up to you, but don't show your faces at my training sessions any more!'

He disappeared into the staffroom.

'And up yours too,' Mickey said, after the door had closed. 'So what does he expect me to do? Cheek me dad? Say "Don't care about your broken toe, I've got to play cricket for the school team"? I'm fed up with the lot of them!'

Sanjay stared gloomily out at a beautiful, soft blue sky, a sky that would have made a perfect dome over a game of cricket. What a terrible waste to have to spend the day packed into a room too small to hold all the guests comfortably.

The traffic was abominable. It seemed as if the whole of England had turned out for Rupa's wedding. When eventually they went into the house it was just as Sanjay had pictured it, teeming with people, particularly full of girls in red saris giggling and screeching. The fire in the paper temple made it even hotter. Sanjay prepared himself for a long stretch of utter boredom. His stomach felt really empty too. There were quite tempting smells of food floating around. If only the ceremony could be over, and they could all eat! While the chanting droned on he was wedged between one of his plumper aunts and his father. He could hardly breathe.

At the moment when Sanjay felt he would last out not a second longer, that he would burst with the heat and boredom and absence of oxygen, the bride and groom emerged from the paper temple, and everyone was smiling and yattering. At last, the food! He wriggled out from behind his aunt, and wondered which table to go to. Would he be with the children or the elders?

And then came the best moment of the wedding, because in the crush he saw Ranjeet near the elders' food table, talking to Rama, and they waved him over.

'Hi man, I hear you're following in the family footsteps. Rama's been telling me about the cricket,' Ranjeet said.

Sanjay tried to look modest, and decided that Rama wasn't too bad a brother after all.

So, the wedding was OK really. On the Monday, though, with the return to school, the misery returned. No chance of cricket practice tonight. His cricket career was over. All Rupa's fault and her wretched wedding.

'They lost!' Mickey said, when Sanjay came into the classroom. 'Smashed, in fact.' There was a note of triumph in his voice.

'Who told you?' Sanjay asked.

'Jason. He was pretty fed up.' Mickey grinned. 'See, they can't do without us.'

'But that doesn't help us,' Sanjay pointed out.

'Oh yes it does. There's cricket practice tonight. How about if me and you just happen to turn up to do a bit of practice on our own? Just sort of minding our own business and not doing any harm. Old Philips might just see how stupid he is to keep us out.'

'OK, but, but we haven't got anything to practise with,' Sanjay said.

'I got a ball I sort of found. We could practise fielding.'

It was too tempting to refuse.

'We better keep to the far end of the field – to start with at any rate,' Mickey said.

Sanjay kept on expecting Mr Philips to come over and bellow at them to clear off, but he didn't. After a while Sanjay forgot about what was happening at the other end as he raced and dived and rolled over to catch the ball that Mickey hurled in his direction.

'They're packing in!' Mickey said. 'Quick, let's go and crawl!'

Mickey hurtled across the ground.

'My dad says he's ever so sorry he messed you about on Saturday,' Mickey said. 'I thought I'd better tell you.'

'He is, is he?' Mr Philips grunted.

There was a little silence.

'My family and I are very sorry too,' Sanjay said, hardly daring to look at the man.

There was another little silence.

'I don't suppose you could give us another chance, sir?' Mickey said.

Sanjay held his breath. This time the pause was

agonizingly long. Mr Philips looked from Mickey to Sanjay. He pursed his lips, gave a deep sigh, and eventually said: 'OK. Just this once. And I mean that. You can come to the next practice. You'd better not cry off ever again. Not even for your grandmother's funeral!'

'Thanks, sir,' they said in chorus, and then belted across the field, anxious to escape.

'Did your father tell you to apologize for him?' Sanjay asked.

'You must be joking! I just thought I'd remind him that it wasn't my fault.'

'That was clever,' Sanjay said.

Mickey grinned. 'Yeah – and the other thing is, like I said – me an' you, we're class! Can't do without us!' He turned off towards his house. 'See ya, Sanjay!'

Sanjay waved, grinning too.

FUN RUN

By Robert Leeson

There are three of us – Scott, built like an ape, Adrian, like a famine victim, and me – neat and medium sized.

Scott's mad. He does things first, then thinks afterwards. Adrian worries. He wouldn't do anything for fear of getting into trouble – if it weren't for Scott.

And they'd both be lost without me. I think things out. I have the ideas. It sounds big headed to say I'm the brains, but, in all modesty, I am.

Take the Fun Run, the school's big outdoor event of the year. Naturally they wait till winter's coming on and it's getting cold and they send you off in PE kit, half naked, running miles up hill and down dale. If you don't get lost or fall off a hill, you crawl in plastered in mud and suffering from hypothermia, to find all the hot water's been used by the idiots who got in first. And they laugh at you. They stand there fully dressed and laugh as you stagger in. That's why they call it a fun run.

And the final insult, it's all for charity.

'The Homeless this year,' said Mr Hipwell, PE thug-in-chief. 'This year we aim to beat last year's total and go over the seven hundred pound mark. Get your sponsor sheets from the office.'

'See the way he was grinning,' I told Scott and Adrian. 'He's a sadist. Imagine him in jackboots. He doesn't care about the Homeless. He just wants to see us suffer.'

'Yer,' said Scott sticking his jaw out. 'He can stuff his Fun Run.'

'Oh, you can't say that,' Adrian began to look worried.

'Hang about,' I took charge. 'We've got to box clever.' I thought for a minute. 'He's got no right to make us, has he? I mean this is supposed to be charity. I bet it's . . .' I had a sudden inspiration. 'I bet it's not in the National Curriculum. And, if it's not, this is illegal.'

They were listening.

'My dad reckons this charity business is a con. The government ought to help the homeless. Little bits of fund raising only make matters worse.'

Well, my dad hadn't said anything about the Fun

Run, but if he had, that's what he'd have said. I know the way his mind works.

Scott's eyes glazed over. They always do when things get complicated. But Adrian's more intelligent. He looked worried.

'So?' said Scott.

'So we go to Hippo and we tell him we're not going. It's voluntary. We don't believe in charity – on principle. And it's outside the National Curriculum.'

'But I do,' murmured Adrian.

'Do what?'

'Believe in charity. I put my spare pennies in a box for – things.' He looked sad. 'I saw this programme on the box, people living in cardboard shelters.'

'Shut up,' we both said. Scott turned to me. 'OK, we go and see Hippo and you do the talking.'

'He'll get mad at us,' worried Adrian.

He was right. Hipwell looked at me from a great height. He ignored the others and seemed to think it was all my idea.

'Underneath that convoluted claptrap about charity,' he bellowed, 'you have the soul of a wood louse . . .'

He put his large ugly face close to mine and hissed. 'I don't care what your father thinks. I don't care what the Secretary of State for Education

thinks. I do not care about your consciences, collective or individual. The Fun Run is compulsory. You, you and you are going to take part and you are going to enjoy it, whether you like it or not.'

Afterwards for some reason the others were cool towards me. But next day, Scott brightened up.

'I've cracked it. We wag off.'

'We'll get caught,' agonized Adrian.

'Not if we box clever,' I took charge. 'My dad reckons that when our school was the Grammar and they used to call it the Cross Country, they used to sneak off down Hangman's Lane. Then they hung about in Brookfield Park while the others ran the full course. They were smart. They didn't join in at the front, but half way like.'

'Right.' Now Scott tried to take charge. He's got this thing about being a leader and he hasn't the intellect. 'We do that.' He stuck his finger in my chest. 'You work out the details.' Then he thumped Adrian on the back and made him swallow his Dental Health chewing gum. 'Don't fret. It'll be a doddle.'

Well, it wasn't. Hippo ran the first mile with us. He wanted to enjoy seeing us struggle up the hill out of town. You could see people looking at us as we staggered past, muttering about life support and other witty remarks. It was very embarrassing.

What made it worse was the other two. Adrian kept saying, 'My mum says I shouldn't run uphill, it's bad for my chest.' And Scott kept asking, 'Where's Hangman's Lane?'

Was it my fault the whole area had been changed since my dad's day?

'They must have renamed it.'

Scott glared at me. 'Right. The moment Hippo goes ahead we slip off that way.' He jerked his head towards the left.

After twenty agonizing minutes when I thought my legs would crumple, Hippo got tired of monitoring us and shot off ahead.

'Now,' muttered Scott. Suddenly he started to hop. 'Oh me . . . foot,' he gasped and staggered out of the ruck. I did the same. Adrian followed us, blushing red and not having the nerve to fake a stone in his sock.

'Right. Lead the way to Brookfield,' Scott told me.

I looked round. There were houses everywhere, all the same. None of the roads led anywhere. How did people find their way?

'This way,' I said quickly and set off with the others trailing behind. One road led into another, more houses, more gardens. No shops, no bus stops. No people. We walked for ten minutes.

Scott stopped. 'You're lost.'

I shrugged. 'So are you.'

Scott raised his hands as if he was going to put them round my throat, then he said: 'Let's ask somebody.'

Adrian looked horrified as Scott marched up a garden path and banged on a door. No answer. Next door was the same. At last, after the fourth try, Scott came back to the road.

'Let's hitch,' he said.

'Oh no,' Adrian was alarmed. 'You don't know who it'll be.'

'Get off,' Scott snapped. He turned and signalled

and to my amazement, a car pulled up. A man with a red face and ginger moustache looked out.

'Whither bound?'

There was something funny about his manner, but I thought quickly and spoke before Scott could muck things up.

'We're on an initiative test, sir.' That seemed to please him. At least he started to grin. 'We have to get to Brookfield Park by two fifteen exactly.'

'By car?'

'That's it. Any mode of transport sir. The main thing is initiative. We get points for being there, not for distance . . . '

'Sounds like cheating to me,' growled the driver. 'Still, times change. Hop in the back.'

We climbed into the back of the car and off he went like the clappers, throwing us over one another.

'I think we've made a mistake, taking a lift from a stranger,' Adrian whispered.

'Shut up,' we told him. I turned to Scott. 'See, we'll be there in five minutes.'

'We're going the wrong way,' whispered Adrian.

'How d'you make that out?'

'He's going uphill. School's downhill.'

'Ah, you worry too much. He's getting back on the main road.' I started to chat up the driver. 'Very good of you to help us, sir.'

'Huh,' he grunted. 'Initiative test eh? In my day we didn't go in for that sort of rubbish. Too much like skiving. We had the Cross Country. Great times, those. Up to the top of the valley round along the ridge to the beacon, then down through the woods.'

'Did you come in first, sir?'

'Ha, first five. Nothing less worth while. We always knew when we got to that park down by the market square that we were on the last lap.'

'That's right, not far from school, sir.' I felt Scott nudge me but ignored him.

'Right,' said the driver, 'quarter of a mile. That's where the skivers used to hang about and try and join in. Of course we never let them get ahead. Little turds. Not likely.'

The car swerved round another corner. Now we were in a country lane, climbing steeply.

Adrian cleared his throat. 'Excuse me sir, but I think you're going the wrong way.'

'Ha,' snorted the driver. 'You think so. Well I'm not. I'm taking you young slugs back to the Cross Country route. I'm going to see you don't get away with it. Cheek,' he muttered.

The situation was dodgy. Some finesse was called for.

'Just drop us here if you like, sir,' I said. 'Wouldn't

be fair to take us right up to where the rest are. We'll catch them up.'

He swung round and glowered while the car waltzed to and fro across the white line.

'Don't try your smarm on me, boy. I'm taking you to the half way mark so you don't sneak back. You're going to finish the course – like men.'

Suddenly Scott wound down the window on his side and stuck out his head. 'Help, help,' he yelled. 'This dirty old man's abducting us.'

It was so crude, I was ashamed. Adrian had almost vanished into the seat, his face crimson. My head banged against the seat in front as the car stopped dead.

'Out,' ordered the driver. 'I might have known.'

We tumbled out on to the grass verge.

'No sporting spirit – typical,' he snarled as the car shot up off the road.

We looked at each other then down into the valley. Town and school looked miles away.

'Come on,' said Scott, crossing the road.

'Where're you going?' I demanded.

'Over here.' Scott launched himself at the stone wall beside the road.

Adrian was still worried. 'We'll get lost.'

'Impossible. Downhill all the way.'

It was. There was a big sloping field, then trees,

then another wall, more grass, soft and slippery. We ran, we tripped, we tumbled, we rolled over and over. We couldn't stop, through grass clumps, thistles, gorse bushes and cow pats, till, hysterical with laughing, we shot over a little cliff and landed in a stream.

'My mum said I shouldn't get wet,' moaned Adrian.

'You'll dry off,' said Scott. 'Come on, follow the stream down. Bound to lead to the river.'

We followed, down the stream bed, from one field to another, dodging under bridges, barbed wire, going down down. Till suddenly a big green bank loomed and the stream vanished.

'We're stuck,' said Adrian. 'We'll have to go back.'

'Give over,' jeered Scott. 'There's a culvert.'

There was too, at the bottom of the bank, a brick tunnel about a metre or so high. The stream poured into the dark and it smelt like death.

'We'll get our feet wet.'

'You won't. Listen. My brother told me. You walk sideways and put your hands on the opposite side. Like this.'

Swiftly, like a crab, Scott disappeared into the gloom. I followed again, and after a bit of mither, so did Adrian. Five minutes later, a bit wet round the edges where we'd slipped on the slimy brickwork, we got out into daylight.

'Look at that!'

In front was a broad green hollow. On one side blackberry bushes climbed the slope, thick with dark berries. On the other there were chestnut trees, dripping conkers. We forgot what we were supposed to be doing, even Adrian, and charged down. We stuffed ourselves with berries and filled our pockets with big, glossy conkers.

We'd have stopped all afternoon, but we were interrupted.

'Hey. You lads!'

Back at the top of the bank over the culvert was a bloke. A big bloke, with a dog, bigger than himself.

'You lot. Come here.'

Adrian went pale. 'I told you we'd get into trouble.'

It was time for me to take charge. I shouted to the man. 'We're not doing any damage.'

Even at that distance I could see his face go deep red.

'You're trespassing, you—' and a number of words followed. The sort you get told off for using in the school yard.

I answered quite reasonably. Dad had told me all about the law of trespass. 'We'll leave by the shortest route.'

'———,' he yelled. Then he let the dog go.

We went down the slope like rockets. Adrian was well in front. Behind us I could hear the dog rasping away like the Hound of the Baskervilles. And I didn't have my service revolver. The wall up at the top of the hollow must have been two metres high but Scott and I went over it like swallows, carrying Adrian with us.

'I've cut me knee,' he howled.

We crashed down on the other side, rolled down a bank and into the road.

'Look at those boys. The things they get up to,' said a voice.

We looked round. We were in the main road, and cars were charging round us, hooting. Behind us was a bus stop, a broken-down shelter and a bench with three fat women, carrying shopping bags. One of them burst out laughing.

'Joe Stanley's been after you with his dog.'

She nudged her neighbours and they laughed as well. Then one called: 'Hey up. Here's t'bus.'

Swinging into the space by the shelter came the little bus with the beautiful words on the indicator: *Hadleigh Market Place.*

Already the women were clambering up the steps. Scott was right behind them. Adrian hung back.

'We've not got the fare.'

'Don't worry,' I assured him. 'We just give our addresses.'

The driver looked funny. 'How do I know it's your address?' he demanded.

I was firm. 'You're forced to accept it, it's the law.'

He fixed me with his eye. 'Any more of that, me lad and your name'll be Walker.'

'Oh, come on Harold,' said one of the women. 'We'll pay for 'em, won't we girls? I can take one child free on me warrant.'

The driver scowled. 'All right. That's one.'

'I'll do another,' said the second woman. 'I'll have the little skinny one with the cut knee. He can come and sit with me, poor love.'

'I'll have the big 'un,' said the third. 'He looks cheeky.'

'Well, I'll have the one that's left,' said the first woman. 'He's not up to much but he'll do. Come here lad,' she told me and patted the seat, well about a quarter of it that was left, beside her.

The bus pulled out into the road and we rolled down into Hadleigh. We were silent, but the women talked all the way.

'What are you lot up to then?' A nudge in my ribs, that nearly sent me into the gangway, told me I was supposed to answer.

I started my spiel about the intiative test, but they all laughed like drains.

'Get off with your bother. You've been on the Fun Run and got tired. My grandson tapped me for fifty pence for it.'

'Well, you can't blame the poor little jiggers,' said my sponsor, scoring a centre against my ribs with her elbow. 'I didn't reckon much to sports when I were a girl.'

'My mum,' announced the second woman, 'wouldn't let me go in for outdoor sports at school – 'cause of my health.'

The others shrieked for some reason.

'You made up for lost time when you left school,' they called. The driver looked round and winked.

'That were indoor sports.'

'You shut up, Harold,' they all howled together as the bus drove into Hadleigh and swung into the bus station by the market. The women, still cackling, rolled away across the square. I turned to Adrian and Scott.

'What did I tell you? I fixed that all right.'

But Adrian wasn't happy yet. 'How we going to get back to school?'

'Easy, quarter of a mile up the road.'

'Yes, but all the kids coming down for the buses'll see us. Look they're coming in now. Hey, we aren't half late.'

He was right. School was well over and first years were streaming into the bus station.

83

'Round here,' said Scott. 'There's a bench. We can wait while they go.'

There was a seat around the corner of the station caff.

'There's someone there,' complained Adrian.

'Plenty of room,' I replied. But that wasn't strictly true.

Sitting in the middle of the bench was an old dosser. Well, he looked old with his beard flowing over his chest. An ancient raincoat stiff with dirt like a cloak covered most of him, except for the frayed trouser ends and broken boots. Plastic bags and boxes took up most of the rest of the seat.

I was just going to ask him politely to make room when the smell from him hit me. I felt dizzy. No wonder there was no-one else sitting there. We couldn't sit down, but we couldn't move off in case the school bus crowd saw us.

'What're you gawping at?'

The voice came from inside the beard.

'Er, nothing.'

'Well, clear off then.'

'We've as much right to stay here as you,' I said with dignity.

The shape on the bench straightened up. Two bloodshot eyes glowed like lamps. A face came into view.

'You've got homes haven't you? What d'you want to pester me for? Shove off.'

'In a minute, when the crowd clears,' I said.

His eyes clouded over. But his forehead got all ridged. It looked as though he were thinking. But I couldn't be sure. Then his shoulders began to shake up and down, till the whole body under the dirty mac was quivering. From the middle of the whiskers came a choking gasping sound. For a moment I thought he was having a fit. Then I realized he was laughing. Next minute he started to wheeze and cough like an old car breaking down. Then he spoke.

'I know what you're up to. You wagged off the Cross. Hey, come and sit down.' He started to shift his gear and, feeling slightly sick, we sat down. Scott managed to sit farthest away. Adrian and I felt as if we were wrapped in a blanket of pong. The old dosser tapped me on the knee.

'We used to. We did all we could to get out of games. We used to pick the spot, go over the wall, lie on the grass or pick berries then get the bus back. There were always somebody soft-hearted who'd pay us fares. Don't suppose it'd work now. Folk are too selfish.'

He gripped my knee. His face turned to mine and his foul breath made me feel queasy.

'It would have been less bother to go on the Cross Country, 'cause we were worn out when we got back. But that never occurred to us. But one year we overdid it.'

His voice died. I thought he'd gone to sleep, but he was thinking: 'One year we nipped off down Hangmans Lane to Brookfield Park, then joined in and came first. That did it. We all got six strokes. Don't suppose they use the cane these days. Country's going to the dogs . . .'

'Hey mister,' said Scott. 'When you came back on the bus how did you get into school without folk seeing you?'

The dosser was spurred into action. He lumbered to his feet, scooped up his gear, and lurched towards the tarred fence behind the bus garage. We stared, then followed him. When we caught up he'd pushed back two planks and was forcing his way through.

Beyond the fence was waste ground. Old houses and workshops had been flattened and left. Rank grass, bushes, small trees had grown up between the brickpiles. A trail of smoke rose behind a half-demolished wall. Here and there in corners of old buildings, slabs of board, old doors and sheets of iron and plastic had been used to make shelters. There must have been a dozen of them. People were living here.

In the shelter of the wall was a fire, a litter of bags, boxes, cans. And around the fire a dozen men and women. As we followed the dosser, a man got up from the fireside and swore at us. But our man stopped him.

'They're with me,' he grunted. The rest glared at us but said nothing.

Now we were over the waste ground and ahead I could see the river. Directly below us was an old lock, water gushing through the broken gates. The tramp pointed. Across the water was more waste ground, then a hedge, and over the top of the hedge in the distance we could see goal posts and the roof of school.

'Back way in. Over the field and across to the gym. No-one ever found out.'

Adrian thanked him. He looked at us without speaking. I felt I should say something.

'Our cross-country. It was a Fun Run – for the Homeless.'

His shoulders started to quiver again, the lines of his face disappeared and he coughed and choked. Then he found his voice.

'Wait till I tell 'em. No wonder you wagged off.'

The awful grating sound started again. We didn't wait now but ran across the lock. Light was fading but I could still see him standing there.

87

Scott peered ahead: 'Waste of time going back to school. I bet it's all locked up over there. Nobody about. I'm off home.'

'Like this?' squealed Adrian pointing to his mud-spattered running gear.

'Dah. Who's going to see?' Scott turned to me. 'We can nip round the side and climb over the gate.'

I was thinking, working out a number of convincing lines I could take when I got home: lost way, abducted by mad pervert, stopped to help old ladies on bus, Task Force visit to Hadleigh's Cardboard City. They all seemed tempting.

'I'll get skinned if I go home like this,' said Adrian. 'I'm going to the gym.'

'It'll be shut up.'

'Might not.'

'Will.'

Adrian's face suddenly changed: 'For once, just once will you two do something I say?'

With that he started over the field, and without thinking Scott and I followed. I realized how stiff and tired I was. As we reached the gym, Adrian signalled excitedly.

'Open,' he whispered. 'They must have forgotten.'

We sneaked in, heading for the changing room. But as we pushed open the inner door, the lights went on. We blinked in the glare as the room filled with a tremendous noise. It was packed with kids and teachers all laughing, pointing, clapping. Some-one started to chant:

'Why were you born so beautiful?'

Why were you born at all?'

I turned to Adrian. I was going to tell him what I thought of his brilliant idea when Hipwell raised his meaty hand.

'All right, all right. A bit of hush please.' Then to us. 'Congratulations. You have broken Hadleigh High School's Cross Country record. No-one has ever been one hour sixteen minutes late before.'

Cheering started. Scott grinned sheepishly. Adrian was one big blush.

'We had the ingenious idea of having a sweep-stake. How late would you be? Denny Harris won and he agreed to put the money back in the kitty. That means you three have raised thirty-seven pounds and twelve pence for the Fun Run and you come top of the list. Congratulations.'

More applause. Scott started to laugh. Adrian sniggered. I couldn't think of anything to say, so I joined in.

WORTH IT

by Malorie Blackman

Monday, 28th June

Old Horsey showed me up something rotten today. Sometimes he can be a right cow pat! After taking the register, he started going through the final selections for the doubles tennis tournament against Lichfield School. His shiny, bald head was bent over the list as he read out the first two teams from our year – Sarah and Minty from Mr Knight's class and Paul and Luther from Mrs Hibbert's class. Then Old Horsey lifted his head and narrowed his eyes and looked directly at *me*. My face started to burn, even before he said anything.

'Judith, if I put you down to play as our C team, can you be relied on to be here, or will you be off school again?'

Everyone turned to look at me. If I'd put my head on my desk at that moment, the desk would have caught fire.

91

'I'll be here sir,' I protested. Old Horsey raised his mega-bushy eyebrows.

'Are you sure? You've been away rather a lot during these last two terms.'

By now all I wanted to do was merge with the paint on the walls and disappear.

'I haven't been bunking off, sir,' I said indignantly. 'It's just that . . . that I didn't feel well. But I've been here for the last four or five weeks. I'm all right now.'

'Hmm!' Old Horsey scrutinized me, his eyes now just tiny slits in his head.

'Do you *want* to play in the tournament?' he asked.

'Of course I do, sir,' I replied. What a stupid question!

'There's no "of course" about it,' said Old Horsey. 'If you turned up to more of the practice sessions, I *might* think you were taking the game seriously. You could be a very good player if only you'd apply yourself. But like everyone else, you don't want to stay after school. Too eager to play video games at home, I suppose.'

Now was that fair or what? 'Don't say a word, Judith. Not one word,' I told myself. Hard work!

It wasn't my fault that I'd been away from school a few times in the last two terms. It's bad enough not being able to set foot in or out of my house unless I play twenty questions with Mum and Dad first, without getting it in the neck at school too.

Take this morning for example.

Dad was late for work, so all he had time to do was down a cup of coffee and pull on his jacket before he headed out the door. But he still found time to interrogate me.

'Are you all right, Judith?'

'Yes, Dad.'

'Are you sure?'

'Yes, Dad.'

'Drinking plenty?'

'Yes, Dad.'

'You're keeping warm?'

'Dad, it's fifty million degrees outside.'

'You're not getting dehydrated, are you?'

'Dad, give it a rest!'

And then I got exactly the same thing from Mum when she drove me part of the way to school on her way to the train station.

The two of them are driving me nuts! And what about that letter they told me to take to Mr Horsmann? I mean, how *could* they? No way was I going to let him or any of the teachers see that. Imagine telling them what I've got and asking them to look after me. I'm twelve, not two. The way my mum and dad are going on, anyone would think I'm about to kick the bucket at any second. We did fine before any of us found out I had Sickle Cell, so why can't we just pick up where we left off? Why does it have to change everything? I'm so cheesed off. All this fuss, fuss, fussing is driving me right up the wall. Tasha's the only one who treats me the way she's always done. Without Tasha I'd go mental, I'm sure I would.

Where was I? Oh yeah!

Anyway, finally Horsey bent his head to his list again.

'OK Judith, you and Tasha are the C team.'

'Yes!' I punched the air above my head. Tasha elbowed me in the ribs, grinning at me.

Old Horsey looked around.

'Class, this tournament is very important. Lichfield School won the cup from us last year and this time next week, I want it back where it belongs.'

'In Mrs Cookson's office where no-one can even glance at it,' Tasha muttered to me.

'Too right,' I mumbled back.

It wasn't as if any of us could just stroll into the head's office and ask to see it. Old Horsey nodded in my direction. 'So you won't let me down, Judith,' he said.

'I won't, sir,' I answered.

Tasha elbowed my ribs again. I elbowed her back.

I crossed my fingers and scrunched up my toes in my shoes. I crossed my arms and my legs. I even tried looking at my nose so I'd go cross-eyed. 'You're not going to get sick again. You're not . . . you're not . . . Not until after the tournament at any rate,' I told myself.

'Judith Stenning, what on earth are you doing?' Old Horsey frowned.

'Er . . . nothing, sir,' I replied, looking straight at him, all innocent.

The frown lines on his forehead were deep enough to swim in but he didn't say anything. Tasha elbowed me for a third time.

'Oi! That hurts, you moron,' I hissed. 'Are you trying to break a bone or something?'

'It was only a light tap,' Tasha said.

Tap, my eyeball! Tasha's 'light tap' has left a whopping great bruise on my side. I just hope Mum and Dad don't see it or, knowing them, they'll want to rush me straight down the hospital.

God, I hate it when they fuss.

★　　★　　★

95

Tuesday, 29th June

I had the strangest dream last night. Maybe it's an omen. I dreamt I was at the tennis tournament on Friday and that our school and Lichfield's were level pegging. Both schools had forty-five points each and there was only one more match left to play. The decider. And guess who had to play it? Yep! Me and Tasha against two of Lichfield's lot.

Everyone gathered around our court. All eyes were on us. No-one said a word. Old Horsey was looking straight at Tasha and me and he didn't even blink. We knew we couldn't make any mistakes.

It was a tough match. It got to one set all and four games all in the third set and then guess what? It was my turn to serve and I served four aces in a row so we won the game. That made Tasha and me five games to four up. Then it was their side to serve. It got to deuce. Then advantage to us. The boy from Lichfield was serving to me and he was *fast*. I could see him winding up for a mega-fast ace. I stepped back a bit. He served. *And I hit it back.* Straight over the net and past both of them. I scored the winning shot. We won the match.

You should have heard the noise then. Our school was screaming and yelling, even Mr Horsmann's eyes were damp. Our school crowded on to the court and lifted Tasha and me up into the air. Mr Horsmann and some of the other teachers started singing some boring song about 'For they are jolly good fellows'. My classmates started singing, 'U can't touch this' and 'In your face'! It was brilliant.

Then I woke up. It was so real, so clear. I felt so good I didn't even mind that it was a dream after a while. It must be an omen. We're going to win on

Friday. And I'm going to have something to do with it. I hope. Maybe.

School wasn't too bad today. Mr Horsmann was more interested in the forthcoming tennis championship than in teaching us anything, which was good because it's far too blazing hot for lessons. He told us that this year, to make sure we get through all the matches before nightfall, only three doubles teams from each year are being allowed to play and each match is only going to consist of one set. Each team gets three points if they win, and one point if they lose. Don't play, no points. That's fair enough. Each team will play three matches. The school with the most points at the end of the tournament gets the cup. I'm looking forward to playing in the tournament so much. I'm sure Tasha and I are going to do well. We're going to be ace!

Tasha and I went for a practice in the park after school. I had to practically go down on my knees to Mum and Tasha had to back me up, but she finally let me go. I swear, she's getting worse. She's almost as bad as Dad now. She gave me a bottle of water to take with me. I ask you!

'If you don't take the water, you can't go,' Mum said.

So I didn't have any choice.

Actually, I was glad after the third game. I felt

like I was wilting, so I was glugging back water like nobody's business. Even Tasha needed some.

I'm glad Tasha knows what I've got. At first I was sorry I'd told her. Tasha's a bit of a div and keeping secrets isn't her strong point. But she's kept mine. I was afraid for a while that she'd tell everyone, but she didn't. I still feel a bit guilty about thinking she'd snitch on me. I should have known she wouldn't. Tasha's not like that.

I think that's enough for tonight. I'm sleepy.

Wednesday, 30th June

Tasha and I went for another practice in the park after school. After a couple of games I called a halt.

'We don't want to overdo it,' I said to Tasha.

'What d'you mean?' she asked.

'Well if we practise too much now, we'll be past our best on Friday.'

'But we've only played two games,' Tasha protested.

'I think we should stop now,' I said stubbornly.

Tasha ran towards the net and jumped over it. She came running up to me.

'Judith, you're not hurting are you?' she asked suspiciously.

'Of course not,' I replied. 'I hope you're not turning into my mum.'

We walked back home and played video games for a while until Dad was his usual subtle self and said to Tasha, 'Haven't you got a home to go to?' Honestly!

I drank a lot of water when Tasha left. I've even got a bottle of water on the floor next to my bed now. I wish it would cool down a bit. I hate it when it gets this hot. Playing tennis in fifty million degrees is all work and no fun.

My stomach started playing up this evening.

Thursday, 1st July

Mum and Dad started on at me this morning. I was trying to eat my breakfast when all the questions started. I sort of lost my temper.

'How are you feeling, Judith?' Dad asked.

'Are you all right?' said Mum.

'Do you have to keep asking me that?' I said. 'If there was something wrong with me I'd tell you. Stop asking me all the time.'

'Judith, we're only . . .'

'You're fussing. I hate it when you fuss over me. I'm not ill all the time, you know.'

By now I was angry. I didn't mean to be but that's how it came out.

'That's enough, Judith.' Mum frowned. 'We're only looking after you. We just don't want you to go back into hospital again.'

I leapt out of my chair. Why did we always come back to that? Ever since last September, when I was told that what was causing my stomach pains and the pains in my arms and legs was Sickle Cell, I'd been in hospital three times – which was three times too often.

I've been ill more times than that, but not bad enough to go into hospital. Which is just as well, 'cause I hate it. All those funny peculiar smells like disinfectant and sick and the doctors talking to me like I was an idiot and the nosy grown-ups visiting their own kids, but still stopping at my bed to ask me what I'm in for. I hate it.

'I'm not going into hospital again,' I shouted. 'I'm tired of hospital. I'm tired of drips in my arm and pethidine injections in my bum and an oxygen mask over my face. I'm tired of hurting. I hate having Sickle Cell. Hate it. Hate it.'

'Judith . . .'

'I've got to go to school,' I interrupted.

And I ran out of the room before Dad could say another word. I grabbed my jacket from off the coat rack and scarpered out the door. I ran and ran, all the way down to the bottom of our road and around the corner. Only then did I give in. I stopped running and clutched my stomach and doubled over. I was almost on my knees with the pain. My eyes were stinging.

'Go away,' I kept saying, over and over.

I couldn't be ill – not now. Not with the tennis tournament only one day away. I just had to hang on for one more day. I forced myself to straighten up. I took lots of deep breaths.

'My stomach doesn't hurt. It doesn't hurt the least bit,' I muttered.

I took one step forward and doubled over again.

'I'm going to play tennis tomorrow. You're not going to stop me,' I told my stomach.

The pain started to ease a bit at that. It really did. It didn't go away completely, but at least I could walk to school now.

I told Tasha that I couldn't practise in the park after school with her because Mum wanted me to come straight home. In the break times and at lunchtime I headed for the nearest water fountain and drank until I felt like a water-filled balloon. Then I made for the library and sat in the coolest bit of it. It was no use. Tasha still found me.

'You *are* hurting, aren't you?' She stood over me, looking really annoyed.

'Don't worry. I'll play tomorrow if it kills me,' I whispered back. 'So you can take that look off your face. I'm not going to let you down.'

'Don't be so stupid, Judith.' Tasha was even more annoyed now. 'If you're hurting, you shouldn't play. It's you I'm thinking about. I couldn't care less about the tennis championship.' She sat down next to me. I glanced around, anxious to make sure that there were no nosy parkers within earshot.

'Tasha, I'll be all right. I just have to take it easy today.'

'You should tell Mr Horsmann . . . '

'No chance. And if you tell him I'll . . . I'll . . .'

'All right, I get the idea,' Tasha said.

We glared at each other.

'So where's it hurting this time?' she asked.

'My stomach.'

'Is it bad?'

'It comes and goes. It's not too bad at the moment.'

'You should tell your mum and dad at least. If you hang about, it'll only get worse,' Tasha said.

I scowled at her. 'What makes you such an expert?'

'You do,' Tasha replied. 'You're nuts! No tennis tournament is worth playing if you don't feel well. Not even Wimbledon!'

'It's not so much the tennis tournament,' I sighed. 'I just . . . I don't want to spend the rest of my life not doing things because of . . . because of what I've got. I've got to prove to myself that I can do anything anyone else can do.'

'So how's playing tennis tomorrow when you don't feel well going to prove that?' Tasha asked.

'It just will, that's all.'

'That's the daftest thing I've ever heard.' Tasha snorted. 'If *I* was ill with the flu or chickenpox or something, I wouldn't play tomorrow. So why do you have to play?'

'Because I do. Besides, it's not the same thing. You only get ill once in a blue moon.' I frowned. 'Tasha, if I don't do this now, there'd be no point in me doing any sports or trying anything new ever again. It's like . . . it's like if I don't play, then I won't do anything because I might get ill. I don't want to have a ready-made excuse that I can use at any time. Once I start doing that then I don't have to try anything, ever again.'

'I don't understand.'

I shrugged. 'Look, I have to play tomorrow. I just *have* to. Besides we're going to win all our matches, I know we are.'

'Oh yeah! And how do you know that?' Tasha asked.

'Don't laugh,' I whispered, 'but I dreamt it. And this dream is going to come true.'

'You dreamt it?' Tasha couldn't believe her ears. I nodded.

Tasha just looked at me and shook her head.

'My partner's gone round the twist,' she sighed. 'That's just great, that is! You're not going to stand on the court tomorrow and say you're a tea pot or a poached egg are you?'

I creased up laughing. That took my mind off my stomach for a while.

I'm going to sign off now. I want to get an early night. My stomach still hurts. I must admit, I'm a bit worried. If the sun blasts down tomorrow like it's been doing all week, then I'm in trouble. Big trouble. But nothing's going to stop me from playing. Absolutely nothing. We're going to *win*.

Friday, 2nd July

I drunk about a pint of water before I went to bed last night, but I still woke up hurting. The pain wasn't too bad. I've been through worse. But it still hurt like hell. I got out of bed and went to have my shower. I'd barely reached my bedroom door, when my stomach let me know that it was there –

with a vengeance. A sharp, stabbing pain shot right through me from my navel to my back. It was so bad it made me yelp out. I bit my lip after that, terrified that Mum and Dad had heard. Luckily for me they were downstairs. I had a quick shower and went down for my breakfast. I forced a smile on to my lips, like painting it on. Mum has this way of just looking at me and knowing that something's wrong, so I couldn't risk that. I forced down my breakfast, even though I wasn't the least bit hungry, just so Mum wouldn't get suspicious. Then I picked up my racket and headed out the door. I groaned the moment I stepped out of the house. It was baking hot already. Something told me it wouldn't be getting any cooler. Tasha was coming up the garden path.

'How are you feeling?' she asked.

'Tasha, if you grew a moustache, I could call you Dad,' I told her. She got the message. She shut up about my health after that and we walked to school together. We talked about the tennis tournament and our strategy for each game we were going to play. Basically, if the ball came in my direction, I'd hit it; if it went towards Tasha, she'd hit it. Not difficult at all!

The tennis tournament was to start after Old Horsey took the register. I was glad about that. I wasn't sure if I'd last until the afternoon. My back had started up as well.

At last it was our turn to play. My stomach was getting worse.

'Judith? Judith, are you all right?' Tasha whispered as we walked out on to the court.

I looked at her. I didn't answer. I spun my racket and we won the toss so Tasha decided we should serve first.

I'm not going to go into all the gruesome details. Except to say that we lost, five games to seven. It wasn't a bad game but it wasn't our best either. What made it worse was that I was sure we could've won it if I'd been feeling better. Old Horsey said as much when we came off the court.

'Better luck next time, both of you.' he said, writing down the scores. Then he looked at me, 'And Judith . . .'

'Yes, sir.'

'Try running for a few more shots. They're not going to come to you, you know.'

'Yes, sir.'

We walked towards the high fence which marked one side of the court where we were to play our next match. Tasha flopped down. Biting down hard on my bottom lip, I gingerly sat down, feeling my way with my hands first.

107

'It's getting worse, isn't it?' Tasha said quietly. I nodded. My eyes were stinging.

'Judith, I don't like this,' Tasha said unhappily. 'You shouldn't be playing.'

'I'll be all right.'

'Not if you keep playing.' Tasha replied immediately.

'Stop fussing. I hate . . . '

'It's not fussing. I'm talking sense,' Tasha interrupted. 'You shouldn't be playing. I've a good mind to tell Mr Horsmann.'

I grabbed her arm. 'Don't you dare,' I warned. 'We have to play. It's too late to find someone else to take my place now, and if we don't play we won't get any points.'

'Stuff the points!' Tasha glowered at me.

'We've only got two more matches to play. We'll win the next two.'

Tasha shook her head, but she didn't say anything. She didn't understand. It wasn't the tennis championship I was so concerned about. I just wanted to play. It was silly, I knew, but I *needed* to play.

We had to wait a while for our second match, and it was almost worth the wait. We had a very close set, but in the end the other team won by six games to three. We shook hands at the end of the match like they do on the telly, then we went to find a seat.

I thought we'd get a rest before our third match but nothing doing. Mr Horsmann told us that our third match was to follow straight on from our second.

My stomach wasn't getting any better.

'Tasha, I don't think I can run much,' I told her as we walked out on court again.

'I knew it. I just knew it,' Tasha said furiously. 'We should stop, right this second. If you explain to Mr Horsmann, he'll . . .'

'No! I'm playing. It's only one more match,' I said.

I remembered the dream I'd had a few nights before. This match we'd win. We had to win just one. And then the cup would be back in our school again.

Tasha and I lost.

No, we didn't just lose. We were thrashed. We were hammered into the ground. We were pulverized. The final score was one game to us, six games to the other pair.

And it was all my fault. I couldn't run for any of the shots, I had trouble lifting my arms to serve . . . Basically, I was a disaster.

So much for that rotten, stupid dream.

We'd lost – all three matches.

At the end of the match, Mr Horsmann came towards us, his face stony. Sweat was pouring off me. I looked and felt like I'd been swimming in my sports kit rather than playing tennis. My heart was thundering and I felt so sick. I had to struggle to stay on my feet.

'Mr Horsmann, Judith doesn't feel well. Can I take her inside?' Tasha said before Old Horsey could get a word in edgeways. Our teacher took one look at me and obviously saw that Tasha was telling the truth.

'Mrs Hibbert, could you take over the scoring?' he called out. Mrs Hibbert came over and took his clipboard with all the scores on it.

'What's the matter, Judith?' Mr Horsmann frowned.

'I've . . . I've got Sickle Cell,' I whispered, 'and I'm having a crisis.'

Mr Horsmann's expression changed at once. 'A crisis?'

'That's what it's called when it starts to hurt a lot,' Tasha explained for me.

'I'll give you a piggy back ride to the medical room. Hop on.' Mr Horsmann squatted down, his back towards me.

I put my arms around his neck whilst he held my legs. Riding on Mr Horsmann's back made me want to laugh, even though my insides were killing me. We must have looked like total divs. Tasha fell into step beside us. I looked around. Every game had stopped as everyone started gawking at us. That made me want to laugh too. Only the pain in my stomach stopped me.

'How long have you been feeling unwell?' Mr Horsmann asked.

'A couple of days,' I replied without thinking. Mr Horsmann turned his head.

'Why on earth didn't you say something?' he

asked. 'What on earth possessed you to play today when you knew you weren't well?'

'You told me not to let you down. You said we should get the cup back,' I reminded him.

'Nonsense! The cup's certainly not worth your health. We could have found someone else. And even if we couldn't, the tournament would still have gone on. It doesn't rely on just one person. That's the whole point – this is a team tournament. And you know as well as I do that it's an annual event. You could've played for us next year.' Mr Horsmann let go of one of my legs and started tapping me on top of my head. 'Is there *any* grey matter up there at all? Judith, I can't believe you were so stupid.'

'That's what I said to her, sir,' Tasha piped up.

'I wanted to play,' I protested. 'I wanted . . .' I gasped as another sliver of pain shot right through me.

'Let's get you to the medical room and then I'll call your parents,' said Mr Horsmann.

After that Mr Horsmann nagged and fussed and fussed and nagged over me until Dad arrived. Then Dad took over where Mr Horsmann had left off. Dad drove me home and helped me to bed. I drank lots of water, took some aspirin and tried to sleep. I almost drifted off a couple of times but that was it.

The pain grew steadily worse and worse. So much for the aspirin! They did no good at all.

Two hours later, I was curled up in a ball, clutching my stomach and howling. Mum and Dad drove me round the hospital where they took me straight in – again.

That's where I'm writing this from. I haven't got much more time because the nurses are going to switch out the lights at any second. This evening Mum and Dad stayed with me until visiting hours were over. I got Mum to phone Tasha at home and tell her where I was. She came to visit me too. Mum and Dad showed me up something rotten.

'Judith, how many times have I told you not to play games if it's too hot?' Mum said. 'Your ears are made out of flint!'

'Her ears are stuck in her backside,' sniffed Dad.

See what I have to put up with, I thought as I looked at Tasha. She smiled at me. Mum and Dad carried on talking to each other about my ears – what they were made of and where they were on my body and such like. Tasha sat on the bed.

'How are you feeling?' she asked. There was that question again. But for once I didn't mind.

'Better now,' I said. 'They've given me some pethidine for the pain and it doesn't hurt quite so much any more.'

'What's pethidine like?'

I shrugged. 'It makes you feel a bit sick, so they have to give you an extra injection for that, but I don't mind. As long as the pethidine stops my stomach from hurting.'

It was strange talking with an oxygen mask on. Cool air was whistling up my nose and when I breathed out, it sounded really loud.

'What's that, then?' Tasha pointed to the upside-down bag of clear liquid which ran down a thin tube and into a vein in my arm.

'It's a drip.'

'I know that. What's in it?'

'Saline I think. Salt water,' I answered.

I moved my arm slightly to watch the drip tube swing back and forth.

'Well?' Tasha asked.

'Well what?' I frowned.

'Was it worth it?'

I looked at the drip and listened to the whistling of the oxygen in the mask which covered most of my face and thought about the pethidine jab they'd given me in my bum.

'All things considered, yes it was,' I said at last. 'It was stupid of me to play, but I reckon it was worth it.'

'Why?' Tasha asked.

'Because . . . because I *played*. Because I was hurting and I still managed to play. Because I tried.'

Tasha shook her head. 'Like I said, absolutely round the twist!' she said. I grinned at her.

'So which school won the tournament? Do you know? Did we win?' I asked.

She grinned back. 'We sure did. It was very close. Our school won by one point.'

GATE-CRASHED

by Brian Morse

He was truly enormous for an infant, tall and broad, with a swagger on him and a way of looking round as if he owned the world. Not that anyone knew he was an infant at that stage. In fact they thought the opposite. He looked quite big enough to be in top class when he appeared in school on Sports Day morning.

'Look. By the door,' Gary growled in Paul's ear. 'Him! Look! Take a look at him!' He nudged his arm.

'Leave off, will you!' Paul was dreaming. He was running the perfect race. Michael Shakespeare from Hyatt House, his rival from the class next door, was trailing him by twenty metres. He let the poor fool gain a metre or two, but just as Michael thought he was fading Paul surged again. The whole school was cheering – everyone – even the headmaster was jumping up and down it was that impressive! Paul breasted the tape! The theme from *Chariots of Fire* flooded the school grounds. From among the applauding parents Sebastian Coe stepped forward to present the trophy.

'Look! *Look!*' Gary insisted. Reluctantly Paul looked up. A lad was at the door leering round at everyone, a large athletic-looking one. 'He's not joining our class, is he?'

'How could he be?' Paul said. 'It's only two weeks to the end of term. Wouldn't be worth it, would it?' Everyone was off to secondary school after the holidays. But you could see why Gary thought it. The lad was so big. Then his mother appeared with him, followed by the headmaster, and it made you want to laugh, she was so small in comparison, a little dot of a woman in a limp summer dress. They watched all three advance on Mr Bellerby's desk and Mr Bellerby look up and go into the smiling mode he kept for visitors. 'Good morning!' he said. 'Good morning!' 'Just keep still!' mother said to son. The son stood to attention.

After a minute or so, however, he began to get restless. He began to poke round the room. The class watched him disgustedly. How could anyone walk into a strange classroom with that much air of owning it? Thirty pairs of eyes watched him finger the open box of Technical Lego in the science corner, sixty eyes saw him slip a connecting rod into his trouser pocket. Of course the adults, deep in conversation, saw nothing. The brat walked his fingers along the shelves, eyes everywhere, grinning to himself, towering above everyone he passed. Then he reached the window. There were other objects in his pocket by now, all tiny useless things. He leaned on the sill. Outside it was sunny, perfect weather for this afternoon. You could still smell yesterday's mown grass. After peering he turned and said very loudly, 'Sports Day, is it?'

Sarah Green, who was closest to him, thought she was being addressed. 'Yes,' she said. Paul sniggered. Why else would the field be covered with flags, and the chairs from the hall be standing in rows by freshly painted white lines? 'This afternoon.' Sarah peered up at him.

'At my school I'm champion runner,' the boy said. He flexed his muscles as if daring anyone to challenge him. Sarah didn't respond. 'Who's your champion?' Sarah was looking down at her work, wanting to get back to it. 'Who's going to win?'

'But there are lots of races, you know,' Sarah said, exasperated. 'Which one do you mean?'

'The Big Race, the long distance.' The boy looked round, savouring the increased attention.

'I'm good at that. The champion.'

'From this class?' Sarah sighed. She turned and looked around. Her eyes focused on Paul. 'Him,' she said. She pointed. 'Paul. He's the fastest runner. I expect he'll win.'

The boy took a couple of steps towards Paul. 'Beat you hollow any day!' he said. 'Are you listening?' The adults turned and the headmaster frowned, perhaps wondering whether he really wanted a voice like that around the school. The brat grinned. 'I'd run you into the ground! Betcha!'

'No chance,' Paul said, as coolly as he could, conscious of the class's eyes on him.

'At my school,' the boy said, 'my old school, I was the fastest runner. I'd leave you standing.' Mr Bellerby grinned across at Paul and winked. Small chance! the wink meant. He'd said at register he'd put a fiver on him to beat Michael Shakespeare, though Paul wasn't sure whether he was joking or not. The brat came and stood over Paul. 'You don't know what running means round here, you don't! Give you a race any time!'

Paul coloured, wanting to stand up and land the idiot one on his nose, then 'Wallace!' his mother suddenly snapped. It was a surprisingly loud sound from such a small woman. 'Shut it, will you!'

'But, Mum—'

'Come over here, away from those children, you and your lip! This instance.'

'Yes, Mum.' As he did so no-one laughed. If Wallace was loud, his mum was even louder. For a moment the class almost – almost – felt sorry for him.

At break time Wallace (what a name!) was out in the playground on his own. There was a line down the middle of playground you were supposed to keep the right side of, but Wallace was neither on one side of it nor the other, zig-zagging from junior territory into infant and back again. He obviously knew how to get on a teacher's nerves! The junior teacher on duty, Mr Sampson, was watching him thoughtfully over the rim of his coffee mug. 'Ready for this afternoon, are you?' he said as Gary and Paul jogged past at a gentle pace – no point in wasting Paul's energy. (Over the other side of the playground Michael Shakespeare, who was from Mr Sampson's class, was doing warm-up exercises of his own.) 'Mr Bellerby tells me you've been in strict training, Paul, early nights, not too much excitement, raw steak and half a dozen egg yolks for breakfast, that kind of thing.'

'A bit of jogging,' Paul said modestly. 'Three miles a night.' He was exaggerating a little, though twice round the Rec had felt a lot more than three miles sometimes, especially when there was something on the telly he'd wanted to watch. Wallace came closer to listen but the two boys turned their backs.

'Most commendable!' Mr Sampson smiled. 'But of course when you're up against a natural athlete like Michael—!'

'Don't tease him, sir!' Gary said. 'He can't take it.

He nearly had a blue fit when that boy—' he looked round for Wallace '—said he could beat him hollow.'

Wallace had headed off again. He was now five metres on the junior side of the line interfering with a second-year game of football. He tore into the middle of a ruck of players, skilfully flicked the ball out from among their feet and set off with it in the direction of the goal. 'Hey!' Mr Sampson suddenly shouted. 'On the right side, you! Haven't I told you already!' Wallace hesitated and lost the ball. 'If you're coming to this school you'd better learn to do as you're told the moment you're told it!' To Paul and Gary's surprise Wallace walked over on to the infant side of the line.

'We thought he was a junior, sir,' Gary said.

'Him? He's top infant. And *stay* the right side! Savvy?' Mr Sampson shouted. 'He's big though, isn't he?' he said admiringly. 'A real giant! He'll tower above me when he gets to my class.' He sighed. 'Bit of a handful though I gather. Last school sounded glad to get rid of him. Trust his mum to dump him on us on a busy day like today.'

'Dump him?' Paul said. 'He's staying? How long?'

'He's supposed to be seeing whether he likes us enough to join us,' Mr Sampson said. 'At least till dinner time.' Paul breathed more easily. 'He and his mother are touring the local sin bins. You know how keen schools are to get their hands on pupils nowadays.' Then, 'Hey' he suddenly shouted, sprinting towards Wallace who'd begun beating up three of the sturdier infants simultaneously. Football, fighting, nicking, Paul thought. He's good at all of them. Maybe it wasn't idle boasting, maybe he could run as well. He was built for it. Though he could hardly put it to the test against an infant, could he? He shrugged the thought off.

'You'll rip my shirt!' Wallace shouted. He wrenched himself out of Mr Sampson's grip. 'I'll tell my dad on you!'

'You do that!' Mr Sampson said cheerfully. 'I was world heavyweight boxing champion when I was younger too.'

'They were picking on me. You're on their side just because I'm new! It's not fair!' Wallace protested.

'More the other way round from what I saw. And shut up, you three!' Mr Sampson told the victims. 'You probably deserved it. Hey! Where do you think you're going!' he shouted for Wallace had taken off across the playground. 'Come back here! I've not finished talking to you!'

'I'm complaining about everyone, especially you,' Wallace called over his shoulder.

'A little lawyer!' Mr Sampson laughed. 'I love it!'

'We'll get him for you, sir,' Gary said. 'Come on, Paul!' He pulled at Paul's hand and began to run. Wallace saw them coming. He began to run too.

'Let him go,' Mr Sampson called.

Paul was glad to. He'd seen Wallace accelerate. He'd almost felt the force of it, like a gust of wind.

Mr Bellerby, Mr Sampson and Miss Smith were talking as they came up the corridor after break. Paul walked just behind them.

'The sheer cheek of him!' Mr Bellerby was saying. 'The staffroom door smashes open and there he is casting his beady eye over us. I thought it was a police raid! I slopped my tea everywhere. You're not telling me at his last school they were just allowed to waltz into the staff room when they fancied it?'

'But what did you say to him?' Mr Sampson said.

'When he announced he was running in the Long Distance? What could I say? That it was only for third and fourth year juniors, that infants weren't allowed to enter, even giants.'

'You ought to have seen his face!' Miss Smith said. 'I thought he was going to throw a real wobbly.' She laughed. 'When you said he could probably make a guest appearance in the egg and spoon I thought he was going to leap across the room and grab you by the throat.'

'He seems to have taken a fancy to the Long Distance,' Mr Bellerby said thoughtfully, 'goodness knows why. He wouldn't stand a chance at his age.'

'He was egging Paul on to race him in the playground,' Mr Sampson said. 'I was hoping Paul would take him up and put him in his place.' Paul kept his head down.

'It's you I feel sorry for, Rose,' Mr Bellerby said. 'He'll be in your class in September if he graces Hall Green with his presence. Still, he and his mother are touring Joseph Edward Cox and Thameside this afternoon.'

'And good luck to them!' Mr Sampson said. 'Fancy having that mother of his as a parent! Have you heard her voice?'

About twenty metres into the race, with Michael Shakespeare second, Paul just behind him, a boy from another house a mile out in front – but he would burn himself out, they both knew – there was a disturbance back at the starting line, shouting, laughter, a wolf-whistle. Michael looked back past Paul. 'It's some kid joining in,' he said. 'He's not even dressed properly.'

'What kid?' Paul didn't look. He wasn't wasting his energy. This was his race. He was going to win it.

'I don't know him.' They raced on, intent on each other, not on what was going on behind. Then the noise grew. Michael looked back again. 'Yes I do! He came round the school this morning, the loudmouth. He's still in his school clothes.'

Paul almost stopped in his track, to look. It was Wallace with Mr Bellerby hot in pursuit, though not hot enough. Mr Bellerby fell over. Paul recovered his step and caught up. 'He's not allowed to enter, is he? Where'd he come from? He isn't supposed to be here this afternoon. It isn't fair!'

'Who cares?' Michael said. 'He's only an infant.'

'But this is our race.'

'Everyone knows that,' Michael panted. 'Now, just shut up.'

But Paul glanced again. Wallace was already catching up with the back runners. As the pack went round the bend and into the straight he was only five metres behind the leaders. The giant infant grinned at Paul. 'Just watch it!' Michael shouted as Paul stumbled against him. 'You'll get yourself disqualified!' Paul didn't care. He felt so angry – it wasn't fair. This had been meant to be his race. Everyone had said so. With a whoop! Wallace came charging past Paul and Michael. 'What the – !' Michael said.

As Wallace caught up with the startled front-runner Michael took off. He caught Wallace up and as they came into the straight neck and neck everyone was cheering and shouting them on. But Paul's legs felt like lead. He began to fall behind. It should have been him and Michael they were cheering, but suddenly here he was, out of the race altogether. For a second time he almost stopped.

Then Michael fell. (Afterwards he swore he'd been pushed. Paul didn't see it that way, though. He just seemed to have missed his stride and fallen over. Or maybe he'd decided he wasn't going to win, so that was a way out of the humiliation of being beaten by an infant.) Whatever happened, Wallace was suddenly out there all on his own.

The crowd fell completely silent. All you could hear was the thud of feet hitting the grass and the grunts of the runners. Then people began to mur-mur. Paul felt that impulse to stop again. He'd go to Mr Bellerby and demand the race should be started again. Without Wallace. Then a lone voice, Gary's, began to shout, 'Paul-Paul-Paul!' At first he was on his own, then suddenly everyone began to join in. 'Paul-Paul-Paul! Paul-Paul-Paul! Beat him! Beat him!'

They'd reached the last bend but one, with about two thirds of the track left. That tick of cold fear that had stopped Paul from racing after Wallace when he'd been overtaken suddenly went. He had plenty of energy left, hadn't he? Surely Wallace couldn't keep it up? However big he was, he was four years younger and he hadn't been in training. Paul began to run. As they left the bend Wallace was only five metres ahead and Paul was steadily gaining. They went into the straight. Slowly slowly slowly the back ahead got closer. But too slowly. An awful thought struck Paul – that he'd let the school down, he'd left it too late.

They turned into the last bend and Wallace looked over his shoulder. The last time he'd done that he'd grinned, but this time he didn't. His face looked drained. Paul felt hopeful again. Out of the bend Wallace was only three metres ahead. Steadily, centimetre by centimetre, Paul was gaining. Down by the finishing line Mr Bellerby and Gary were holding the tape across the track, Gary dancing up and down in excitement. Two metres between them now and the line only fifteen metres away. Was there time to do it? Wallace glanced over his shoulder, his face distorted with effort. Only a metre and a half now. He could do it, do it! For a fraction of a second Paul was distracted by someone pushing through the crowd on the right, someone small in a summer dress he thought he ought to recognize, but he didn't have time for things like that. He looked straight ahead and ran and ran and ran.

There came this terrible voice. 'Wallace! Come here at once!' and Wallace's mother had materialized on the track. 'I've been looking all over for you, you stupid boy! I've had to run all the way down from the other school.' Ahead Wallace faltered and almost stopped. He veered to one side. 'Wallace! They'll never have you in any school if you don't learn to behave yourself. Come here this moment!'

'Mum! Mum!' Wallace wailed. 'Mum!' It only took that one wrong step for Paul to catch up. His legs were beginning to fail, they were turning to jelly, his lungs felt as if they'd burst, but he ploughed on and on and on. He fell through the tape.

'I think you'd still have beaten him,' Mr Bellerby said as he gave Paul a hand to stand up. 'You had the measure of him. What do you think?'

'Yes,' Paul gasped.

'I don't know why you kept stopping,' Mr Bellerby said.

'No.'

'But I might change my mind about not wanting him in the school.' The teacher pointed. 'Look at him now! He runs like an angel!'

Paul stared through the sweat running out of his hair and down into his eyes. Wallace was still running, running as fast as anyone that afternoon, and keeping it up, metre after metre after metre. Across the centre of the track he went, through the straggle of spectators over the other side, leaping a chair as he did so, away away away towards the far side of the field. Then he doubled back towards the laughing spectators. Every few metres his mum made a grab for him.

'We'll have to conquer his fear of his mother though,' Mr Bellerby said. 'Or maybe we could put it to good use.' He looked thoughtful. 'Olympic champions have been made of stranger stuff.'

It wasn't very nice, but Paul prayed for Wallace's mother to catch him up, prayed, prayed, prayed.

BACK HOME

by Jean Ure

'And then, of course, there's maths,' said Jo. She pulled a face. 'Maths is really gruesome. It's my worst subject, almost.'

'Back home,' said Aileen, 'we don't call it maths.'

From the far side of the room, where Aileen couldn't see her, Matty mouthed, '*Back home*', and waggled her fingers by her ears. Jo, struggling to be polite and friendly as her mother had instructed, said brightly, 'So what do you call it? If you don't call it maths?'

'We call it math,' said Aileen.

'*Math*,' mouthed Matty.

Jo did her best to ignore her. It was all right for Matty: her mother wasn't the one who'd said to go and introduce herself to their new neighbours.

'They've just come over from America. They've got a daughter the same age as you. She'll be going to school with you next term. I think it would be rather nice if you called round and introduced yourself. Try to make her feel at home.'

Jo had spent nearly half an hour trying to make Aileen Foster feel at home. It was an uphill task. Aileen seemed very determined *not* to feel at home. Of course Jo realized it must be strange for her, being in a foreign country, she realized one had to make allowances, but she couldn't help feeling that Aileen might at least have come half way to meet her.

'What about games?' said Jo. 'Do you like games?'

'You mean like Chinese checkers, or something?'

'Um . . . no. More like team games, sort of thing.' What team games did Americans play? 'Football, and—'

'You mean sport,' said Aileen.

All right; sport. Anything for the sake of good relations.

'Do you play netball?'

'Basketball,' said Aileen. 'Netball's for kids. I heard about netball. I have this friend came over here. She said it's a really dumb kind of game.'

Jo swallowed. (Matty, unseen, stuck her fingers up.)

'Well, anyway,' said Jo, valiantly, 'it's nice

you're going to be here for the summer term.
Summer term ga— I mean sport – are really good. I
mean, *is* really g—'

'Back home,' said Aileen, 'we don't call them
terms, we call them semesters.'

Matty rolled her eyes. Jo, striving to be patient,
said, 'OK.' (If Aileen wouldn't speak their language, she supposed they would have to try and
speak hers.) 'We'll call it a semester. Like I was
saying —' Matty glared at her '— we do really good
sport in the summer semester. We do cricket and—'

'Back home,' said Aileen, 'we don't—'

'I know,' said Jo, quickly. 'Back home you don't

135

do cricket. But don't worry, there's lots of other things. There's swimming, and there's tennis, and there's rounders – rounders is one of my favourites. You'll like rounders. At the end of t— I mean, semester – we have the inter-house rounders rally, which last year we *won*.'

'Yes, and Jo scored the highest number of rounders,' said Matty.

Jo went a bit pink. She was proud of her achievement, but it did sound rather like boasting.

'Matty was in the team, as well. Perhaps you might be in it this t— I mean semester. You look as if you'd be good at rounders.'

She only said it to be polite. Aileen didn't look in the least as if she would be good at rounders. She was pretty but flabby, with a quite enormous bottom. She reminded Jo of a postcard Jo had once seen, which had a picture of a girl saying her prayers: 'Thank you, God, for a nice face, but the fat bottom has got to go.' A giggle shot out of her before she could stop it. Matty and Aileen both looked at her in surprise.

'Sorry,' said Jo. 'Got something in my throat.'

And then she felt mean. Aileen couldn't help having a big bum and one oughtn't to laugh at people just because of the way they looked. 'If you like,' said Jo, 'Matty and I could take you down the park and give you a bit of coaching, so's you'd know what you were doing. It'd be fun, wouldn't it—' she appealed to Matty, standing transfixed with horror behind Aileen '—if we all got into the team?'

'I don't want to get into any rounders team!' Aileen tossed her head. She had a long blond pony tail which swished to and fro. 'I know all about rounders. My friend told me. She said it's just baseball without the kicks.'

Jo felt her face grow red and hot. She had been quite prepared to take Aileen down the park and spend hours, even days, if necessary, teaching her how to play. And that was all the thanks she got! It was Matty who took up the cudgels.

'You ever seen rounders?' she said.

'I don't have to see it. My friend saw it. She told me. It's for juveniles.'

'So what do you think you are?' screamed Matty. 'An old age pensioner?'

'Back home,' said Aileen, 'we don't call people—'

Mercifully, at that point, the door opened and Aileen's mum came in with a tray of Coke and biscuits.

'How's it going?' she said. Aileen's mum, unlike Aileen, was grateful to Jo and Matty for taking the trouble to call round. She'd said so, to Jo's mum. 'It's really good of Jo and her friend to take the trouble. It'll make such a difference for Aileen, I know it will.'

Mrs Foster smiled, happily. 'All getting on OK?'

'They want me to play kids' games,' said Aileen. 'Rounders, for heaven's sake!' Aileen swished her pony tail. 'Just baseball without the kicks.'

'Now, come on, honey.' Mrs Foster chucked her under the chin. 'Remember your manners. Jo, Matty . . . help yourselves.'

It was a pity Aileen was so nasty when Mrs Foster was so nice. As they left, Jo and Matty – showing off their British manners – politely thanked her for the Coke and biscuits.

'Back home,' said Aileen, 'we call them cookies.'

Later that day, Fij rang, eager to hear about the new girl.

'What's she like?'

'She's got a fat bottom,' said Jo.

'Is she going to fit in?'

'Not unless she changes her attitude.'

'Why? What's wrong with her attitude?'

'I asked her if she'd like to learn how to play rounders and she said rounders was for juveniles . . . just baseball without the kicks.'

There was a shocked silence, then: 'She said *what*?' said Fij.

Jo repeated it.

'You wait till I tell Barge!' said Fij.

Barge was the leader of their gang at school. She was also one of their star rounders players. She wouldn't take kindly to some foreigner coming over here and jeering.

Jo's mum, who had overheard the telephone conversation, said, 'I hope you remember that Aileen is away from home and probably feeling rather insecure.'

'That doesn't give her the right to be *rude*,' said Jo.

Five minutes later, Barge was on the phone.

'I have just heard,' said Barge, 'from Felicity. She has told me about this person – this creature – this *thing*. *Daring*,' said Barge, 'to come over here, *to our school*, and insult one of our great national games! I have never,' said Barge, huffing down the telephone, 'heard anything like it. It is the very acne of bad manners.'

'Yes,' said Jo. It was. The very acne. (Any other time she might have pointed out that acne was spots and that what Barge really meant was acme, but such a correction would have seemed piffling in the circumstances.) 'I even offered to teach her and she just threw it in my face.'

'Don't you worry,' said Barge. 'We'll teach her all right.'

'But she doesn't want to be taught! She says it's for juveniles!'

'Juveniles!' spluttered Barge. 'The cheek of it! You just wait! We'll show her!'

'Don't see how.' Jo said it glumly. A small reluctant part of her was beginning to wonder if perhaps Aileen was right – if rounders really was just baseball without the kicks. Not that that was any excuse for being rude enough to say so.

'You leave it to me,' said Barge, grandly. 'I shall devise one of my plans . . . '

Barge's plans were never without their complications.

'If you ring Nadge and I ring Bozzy, then Nadge can ring Gerry and Bozzy can ring the Mouse, and Gerry can ring the Lollipop and the Mouse can ring Emma—' Barge was never happier than When she was organizing things. 'If everybody rings somebody, then all you'll have to do is persuade that fat-bum American. Which I am sure,' said Barge, in honeyed tones, 'is not beyond your capabilities.'

'I'll try,' said Jo.

'Just tell her,' said Barge, loftily, 'that if she doesn't turn up we shall know that all Americans are lily-livered cowards.'

Not having Barge's gift for plain speaking,

Jo didn't put it quite as bluntly as that.

'We've arranged this rounders match,' she said, 'to show you what it's really like. We can't help feeling,' said Jo, 'that your friend that came over here must have played some other kind of game, like—'

'Like ring a ring of roses,' said Matty.

'So what we thought was, if you'd like to come along and have a go—'

'If she's not too scared,' said Matty.

'Scared?' said Aileen. 'Of a kids' game?'

Punctually at two o'clock the following afternoon, Jo and Matty knocked on Aileen's door.

'Well, now, so you're all going off to play a game of rounders,' said Aileen's mum. 'Isn't that nice?'

She beamed at them; a big sunny beam, full of gratitude. Jo felt a small stab of guilt, but it didn't last long. Aileen *deserved* to have some of the stuffing knocked out of her.

They reached the park to find that Barge had done her usual excellent job as organizer. The square had been marked out, with four garden forks upended and stuck into the grass to serve as posts, while fifteen members of Year Seven, all kitted up, stood waiting, ready for the off. There was Fij, in a fencing mask, Bozzy in her riding hat. The Mouse had a balaclava, Nadge had a crash helmet. Everyone had pillows pushed up the front of their sweaters and towels or cotton wool stuffed down their socks. Some people wore cricket pads as well. Barge, who was hefty enough to begin with, appeared to have left the coat hanger in her coat. She came swaggering up sideways, being almost too broad to walk head on.

'How do you do?' she said graciously to Aileen. 'My name is Margery, but you may call me Barge and I will call you Ail. Now listen, Ail, I have put you to play with Jo for the Nelligan Kneecappers – Nelligan being the house that we are all in. We do *so* hope,' said Barge, oozing in a treacly fashion, 'that you will be in it with us. I myself am going to be captaining the opposition, otherwise known as the Shapcott Sharks. It's just a friendly game,' said Barge, baring her teeth, 'so no need to worry.' She walloped an uncertain-looking Aileen on the back with a large rubber-gloved hand. 'We're not expecting any teeth to be knocked out today!'

'Ha ha ha!' laughed Fij and Bozzy to show that it was a joke.

'Ho ho ho!' laughed Jo and Matty.

'Barge is so funny,' gushed Jo, opening the sports holdall she had brought with her and tipping the contents on to the ground. 'Do have a chest protector and make yourself some leg guards.' She handed Aileen a pillow and a roll of cotton wool (pillow from Jo's bed, cotton wool filched from the bathroom cabinet). 'When we play at school we have proper body armour, but they're so mean, they won't let us borrow it for friendly games so we're having to make do.'

'But it's all right, we're not using the steel ball,' said Matty, fitting an old metal colander over her head and tying it beneath the chin with a shoelace threaded through the handles. 'Just a rubber one.'

'Rubber, huh?' Aileen, who had fallen rather silent since entering the park, now perked up and swished her pony tail. 'This is kids' stuff compared with baseball!'

'Oh, well, yes,' said Jo. '*Base*ball . . . I expect in *base*ball they have far worse injuries than people just being knocked unconscious or getting their legs broken. Do stuff loads of cotton wool down your socks. Barge is an absolute demon bowler. And look, here are some gloves and something to wear on your head.' Solemnly she held out an ancient frying pan without its handle. 'If you tie this tea towel round it, it should keep it on all right.'

'Is all this junk really necessary?' said Aileen. She gave a little laugh. 'I mean, a rubber ball . . .'

'Oh, yes,' said Jo. She crammed a bobble hat on to her head. 'It's against the law to play dangerous games without some form of protection. Look! The captains are going to toss the bucket to decide who gets first kill.'

Nadge in her crash helmet, and Barge, wearing her coat hanger and cushions, stood facing each other over a dilapidated metal bucket with no bottom. Fij in her fencing mask stood nearby holding a rounders bat.

'When the bat drops,' said Jo.

The bat dropped. Instantly, Nadge and Barge dived for the bucket. Nadge, being the nimbler of the two, got to it first, but Barge, being the heavier, threw her with a cross buttock, seized the bucket and with a yell of triumph hurled it into the air. Aileen screeched as it bounced off her frying pan headgear, but the screech was lost in the rising chant of 'Kill! Kill! Kill! Kill!' coming from the Sharks. For a moment it looked as if there might be a pitched battle there and then, but Fij snatched up her bat and beat at the bucket and Nadge shrieked, 'So they have first kill! What do we care? We'll kneecap the lot of 'em!'

There was some discussion as to where the American visitor should be placed in the field. For Aileen's benefit, Jo listed the positions: 'One chucker, one backstabber, four pitchforks and three ditches – first ditch, second ditch, last ditch.' She and Barge had spent hours on the telephone making up the names. 'The batsmen are called sloggers. This is the slogging square. What you have to do, you have to slog the ball and run as fast as you can round the pitchforks before someone can bring you down. If you manage to get round, then you've scored a rounder. So it's quite simple, really. It's just a question of which position you want to play.'

Nadge said that as Aileen was new to the game she'd better be sent out to last ditch. Matty disagreed. She said that since rounders was only for juveniles, and was just baseball without the kicks, she ought to be given something more exciting such as backstabber.

'I mean, she's used to dangerous games, aren't you?'

'Sure,' said Aileen, sounding rather doubtful. 'But I wouldn't want to spoil the fun for you guys.'

'You won't spoil our fun,' said Matty. 'We want you to enjoy yourself.'

The game began. Barge, as first slogger for the Shapcott Sharks, stepped up to the slogging square. Nadge, playing chucker for the Kneecappers, spat into her right hand, encased in a boxing glove, drew her right arm back, gave a bloodcurdling shriek and hurled the ball as hard as she could, straight at Barge. Barge slashed and missed. The ball slammed into Aileen's unprotected shoulder. Aileen yipped. A great cheer went up from the opposing side.

'That hurt!' said Aileen.

'Ho ho ho!' roared the Shapcott Sharks.

'All part of the game,' said Barge, wrestling with her pillow as she reached third pitchfork.

'Of course, I know it's not baseball,' said Jo.

Aileen swallowed and hunched down again as Bozzy, in her riding hat, squared up to Nadge.

Thwack! went Bozzy, catching Aileen a sharp crack on the wrist with her rounders bat. Aileen howled in agony. No-one took the least bit of notice. Bozzy had tipped the ball and was off, like a rabbit out of its hole.

'Kill, kill, kill!' chanted the Sharks in unison, as Bozzy tore round the pitch. She was almost at fourth pitchfork when Matty, quite casually, stretched out a foot.

'Aaaarrrghghgh!' went Bozzy, turning somer- saults.

One down and eight to go . . .

The Lollipop stepped up to the square. Really, it was impossible to miss the Lollipop, especially with a pillow stuffed up her front and cushions strapped to her hips. Nadge scored a direct hit: the Lollipop retired, winded.

'Out, out, out, out!' chanted the Kneecappers.

Aileen rubbed at her wrist and massaged her shoulder and clamped her frying pan more firmly on to her head. Jo sent her a sympathetic glance.

'Don't worry,' hissed Jo. 'Things'll start to warm up soon.'

Aileen smiled, rather wanly.

After a bit of murmuring amongst the Sharks, Melanie came tittuping out. True to her image as leader of fashion, Melanie wore royal blue ski pants, hockey pads and quilted jacket. On her head she had a plastic bowl, fetchingly secured with a floaty sort of scarf tied in a big bow beneath the chin.

Melanie took up a languishing position, right hand drooping as if she were royalty. Nadge spat into her boxing glove and delivered, fast and deadly, straight for the body. Melanie gave a little squawk and sidestepped – not quite fast enough. Zompf! went the ball into Melanie's thigh. Melanie screeched and dropped her rounders bat. The Kneecappers hooted. Aileen pounced on the ball and looked for something to do with it. Did you hit people with it, or what? Melanie, meanwhile, urged on by cries of encouragement from her own team – '*Run*, bonehead!' – floated off, with what dignity she could muster, towards Jo, at first pitch-fork. Jo jumped up and down, frantically waving her arms at Aileen.

'To me, to me!'

Aileen, half blinded (her frying pan having temporarily slipped its moorings and settled rakishly over one eye) flung the ball in the general direction of Jo. *Clonk*! went the ball, catching Melanie a smart blow on top of her plastic bowl. Melanie screamed.

'Way to *go*!' yelled Aileen, shoving her frying pan back on her head.

The Kneecappers yodelled and punched the air with their fists. Jo scooped up the ball and banged it down triumphantly on top of her upturned fork. Melanie departed, in a dudgeon.

'Nobody said it was going to be like *this*.'

Fij stepped on to the square, peering out through the mesh of her fencing mask. *Wallop*! went Fij, taking a swing. The ball looped out towards last ditch. Fij, long-legged, set off at a gallop. The Sharks cheered her on – 'Way to go, way to go, way to go!' They didn't know what it meant, but it sounded good. Last ditch, who was totally useless, clawed up the ball and feebly lobbed it back towards Matty, at fourth pitchfork. The ball fell with a pathetic plop metres away from anywhere. As Matty rushed out to get it, Fij cantered on, heading for a rounder.

'Way to go, way to go, way to—'

The chant stopped, abruptly. Aileen, with a yell

quite as bloodcurdling as anything Nadge could manage, had suddenly hurled forward and thrown herself at Fij in a rugby tackle. The Sharks stood in awed silence as Fij came crashing down. A cheer went up from the Kneecappers. Two of the local lads, who had come to sneer, stared slack-jawed as Matty joyously hurled herself into the fray. Fij emerged with one sleeve ripped off and a dent in her fencing mask.

'This is my cousin's,' she said. 'He's going to kill me!'

'People who live in glass houses,' chortled Aileen.

Jo giggled, a trifle nervously. Barge hrrumphed down her nose. The idea had been to *humiliate* the creature. She wasn't supposed to join in.

'C'mon, c'mon!' Already Aileen was hunkering back down. She had got the hang of things now: it wasn't so much a game as a battle. 'Move it, move it! What're we waiting for?'

Gerry swaggered on, looking confident. Two seconds later she was hobbling off, kicked on the shin by an over-confident Aileen.

The Mouse came on. The Mouse was deceptive: she looked small and sweet but could be vicious. She managed to reach third pitchfork, having head-butted Jo, punched Matty in the eye and brought

Lee to the ground, before a maddened Aileen came charging to the rescue. The two local lads, drawn in spite of themselves, edged closer to the danger zone.

'What's this, then?' said one. 'Baseball?'

'Baseball?' brayed Aileen. 'You have to be joking! Baseball's kid's stuff compared to this! This is war, man!'

Emma came in and went out again as quickly as she had come. The wicker bread basket which had been skewered to her head with hair grips was now flattened and frayed.

'I dunno what my mum's going to say,' grumbled Emma.

Aileen cackled. 'If you can't take the heat, get outa the kitchen! Next guy, next guy!'

The next guy was Naomi, but Naomi had suddenly remembered that she had an appointment at the optician.

'She'd let a little thing like that stop her?' marvelled Aileen.

Now there was only Barge, the sole survivor of her side: the only one who had not been mauled, tripped, punched, kicked semi-conscious or sat upon. The only one who had got round and lived to tell the tale.

'OK, OK!' Aileen settled down on her big red

tracksuited haunches, rubber gloves at the ready. 'Here's waitin' for ya, buster!'

Barge cleared her throat.

'You are never going to believe this,' gurgled Barge, 'but thanks to Naomi I have *just* recalled that I have the most *urgent* appointment with my dentist . . . two wisdom teeth and a handful of molars,' babbled Barge. '*So* inconvenient – just as we were getting into the spirit of things. Pray accept my most abject apologies. Such a terrible shame, when the real excitement was yet to come. Oh, I do assure you!' said Barge. 'You ain't seen nothing yet, bud – as I believe you say back home. But there you have it, that is life. And now, if you will excuse me, you know how it is . . . wisdom teeth and molars,' said Barge, attempting a witticism, 'wait for no guy.'

Barge fled, followed by her team. The victorious Kneecappers divested themselves of their frying pans and their colanders, their pillows and their cushions, and slowly hobbled their way home. Jo, still striving for politeness, accompanied Aileen to her front door. Aileen had the start of a black eye, Jo was mopping a bleeding nose. Matty limped behind them, nursing a bruised ankle.

'Land sakes!' said Mrs Foster, throwing open the door. 'Did someone attack you?'

'We've been playing rounders,' said Aileen. 'That is some game! You wait'll I tell the kids back home, they'll go wild. I'm really looking forward to playing it next semester, I mean term. I can't wait!'

Jo and Matty eyed each other.

'Yes – well – it mightn't be *quite* the same as it was today,' said Jo.

'No sweat!' Aileen clapped Jo on the back: old buddies. 'I can handle it . . . the tougher the better. Baseball? Huh!' She snorted. 'Baseball's got nothing on rounders!'

THE JUMP

by Anthony Masters

I'll run away then, thought Rik as he lay on his bed, his skateboard on the table at his side. His most treasured possession, painted in red and silver but beautifully battered, it was a really fast deck, and he seemed to spend most of his waking hours on it. He thought about skating all the time, and he and his mate Gus were always trying new moves on the wall. They'd mastered the rock 'n roll, the air, the railslide, but there was another one left – one that had defeated them both. The jump was too big, too dangerous, too terrifying for them, but Rik planned different ways of tackling it all the time.

Of course it would serve them right, he thought. They'd wonder where he'd gone – maybe get the Old Bill after him. But they wouldn't find him, for at ten Rik knew his way around all right; living in Vauxhall had made it easy for him to know London and its skate parks really well. Nowadays they often went to the South Bank; near the Festival Hall there was a rabbit warren of jumps amongst the wilderness of concrete. He'd go up there, he decided, skate all day, live rough at night like the homeless people in Cardboard City. That would show his parents a thing or two and make them *really* miss him.

Life had been OK until the baby came along. Helen. It wasn't that he hated her – in fact he had loved her from the start, with her little helpless cries and wriggling limbs – but they loved her more than him. In fact they had stopped loving him completely; Rik was sure of that.

Rik was going through a bit of a crisis anyway, for he had begun to test out his parents, which wasn't going down at all well. He had been adopted by them when he was four – when they didn't think they could have a baby, he thought grimly. Then a couple of years ago they found they could. It wasn't fair.

Rik had a hazy memory of his earlier life with his real mum, sometimes in the council house in Clapham, or more often in the children's home at Wandsworth. He hadn't spent much time at home, and when he was there Mum was usually drunk or had some guy in. In the end they had taken him away and people came to look at him in the home, bit like as if they were shopping at Tesco, he supposed.

He could remember being very afraid when he had first been adopted and had come to live in the big Victorian flat in Vauxhall, but slowly a history of memories built up with his new mum and dad and he more or less forgot the old life. For a long time it was great; days at Hastings with Mum in the week, football in the park with Dad at weekends, family trips to the cinema, to the swimming pool, to the bowling alley; just the three of them, and it had been good. But now Helen was here and they were four and it wasn't good any longer. The past eighteen months had been lousy with him being shunted more and more into the background.

He had been interested in skateboarding anyway, but directly Rik found he wasn't wanted, it became the central focus of his life – and his school work suffered accordingly.

'Rik!' his mother yelled up the stairs. 'You'll be late. Get on with it!'

Reluctantly he levered himself slowly off the bed and went downstairs, carrying his skateboard. Rik had already made up his mind that he wouldn't go to school that morning. He'd run away instead.

Perhaps it was because Rik *wanted* to make things worse that everything was so dreadful that morning. First of all he dumped his deck on the floor and Mum stepped on it. In fact she did rather more than that; going completely out of control, with one foot on the deck and the other on the floor, she went into a kind of rattling glide, hit the wainscotting and fell on her back.

'You all right, Mum?' said Rik, laughing and spitting out bits of toast. 'I thought you were trying for a rock 'n roll.'

But she didn't see the funny side of it, and from the look of him neither did Dad.

'That wretched board,' said Mum, struggling to her feet. 'It's going to be the death of me.'

'That's it.' Dad stood up and grabbed the deck. 'That's it then.' He held it in his arms as if it was alive. 'I ought to smash this into a thousand pieces.'

Rik was on his feet now, all laughter forgotten. Dad was in one of his rages and he could be really heavy in one of those.

'Don't, Dad.'

'You've been told not to bring this thing in the house.'

'It's not a thing!'

'Don't be lippy!'

'Give it back!' yelled Rik.

'I beg your pardon, young man?'

'I *said* give it back.'

'Right. It's confiscated.'

'I'll be late for work,' wailed Mum in the background. 'And Helen – she'll be late for her minder. Knock it off, you two.'

Rik was jumping up at his dad like an angry terrier and his dad was holding the skateboard aloft as if it was a trophy.

'Give it, Dad.'

'Get off.'

'It's mine!' Rik managed to grab the edge of his deck and pulled as hard as he could. For a moment it was deadlock, and then Rik wrenched at it again; he caught his dad off balance and he staggered back against a chair. Meanwhile Helen howled as if her lungs would burst.

Rik grasped his prize possession to him and ran through the living room, knocking Mum's purse off the sideboard, and was out into the hallway in seconds.

'Come back,' Dad roared as he thundered behind him. Rik tore at the bolts of the door and for a moment thought the top one was going to stick.

'You'll pay for this.' Dad swiped at him and missed, while Rik pulled open the door and legged it. Then he paused halfway down the garden path and waved his deck at his infuriated father as he stood on the front step.

'I'm not coming back,' Rik bawled.

Dad paused, suddenly realizing that he had gone right over the top. 'Now wait a minute.'

'You'll be sorry!' Rik choked back his angry tears, determined not to give in. 'You'll be sorry when I don't come back. Ever,' he added ominously.

'Let's talk.' Dad was uneasy now, prepared to call a truce, but it was too late.

Rik turned on his heel, but not before he had noticed old nosy Nora Norton twitching at her curtains next door. He gave her a rude sign and ran.

His bravado lasted the walk to the South Bank, but by the time he was almost there, Rik felt deflated and his anger, which had kept him going, had turned to despair. His parents had made him promise never to skate alone, but now he was breaking that promise. They didn't want him. They preferred Helen. No-one cared if he ran away.

But directly he arrived amongst the concrete ramps the jump took over, because it both terrified and fascinated him. He'd never been able to do it and neither had Gus. Nor had any of the bigger boys they had both watched.

Last weekend, Mum and Dad and Helen had come up to watch Rik attempt the jump. He was light and small for his age and thought he had a chance because they were there and he was desperate to show them he could do it. But in the end he had failed, and Dad had put his arm round him, in front of all the skaters, and said, 'It's OK, love – you'll do it when you're bigger.' He had never felt so humiliated in his life and he was sure he could hear muffled laughter. Even Gus had grinned.

But now, as Rik looked at the jump again, all his misery left him. In fact, as usual, he didn't think – couldn't think – of anything else. There was a ramp that ran sheer up a rough concrete support that had never been finished, a short bumpy surface and then at least a four metre drop. It was terrifying, but Rik was convinced that if he got up enough speed he could leap the gap and land on another concrete surface that was narrow and lower. He was sure it was possible, although he had seen many other kids come to grief on it. Either they couldn't make the gradient on the first ramp and simply slid back again, or they actually took off, only to plunge into the abyss. He had done this several times himself and had horribly jarred and scraped himself, but another bigger, heavier boy had broken his leg.

A few yards away the Thames flowed swiftly past, winking and gleaming in the October sunshine. The underneath of the walkways was in shadow, as it always was, and full of graffiti and litter. It smelt of old blankets and bodies and other smells that were more unpleasant and less definable. But Rik noticed none of this. He only had eyes for the jump, and as he sized it up for the hundredth time, Rik felt the familiar stirring of butterflies in his stomach. His mouth went dry, his hands and legs shook and the sweat stood out on his forehead. He was dead scared and knew that what he wanted was that extra bit of courage, the extra confidence that would really make him go for it. Then Rik had a brainwave.

Running away was just what he had needed. What he would do now was practise – all day long if need be – until he made the jump and perfected it. Rik knew that a one-off would not be enough. He had to get it absolutely right so that he could make the jump time after time after time. Then he would ring Gus, tell him where he was and command him to bring his parents up to the South Bank. When they were all there Rik would make his jump to an admiring audience. He could see it now: Mum frightened at first but then building up confidence as he succeeded time after glorious time, her eyes sparkling like the river – just as they had sparkled at him before baby Helen came along and wrecked everything. Dad would be amazingly proud of him and really sorry he had been so horrible. He would shake his hand and not put his arm round him in front of the other skaters. Baby Helen would gurgle with delight and hold out her arms to him and Gus would simply say, 'That was rad.'

The only trouble was that he had to do it first, and the imaginary applause ringing in Rik's ears died away. He stared up at the ramp. As usual it looked impossibly high but this time, because it was a weekday, there was no-one around to provide any competition. Not wanting to waste any time, Rik walked away, got on his deck and built up as much speed as he could, the wheels rasping on the scarred concrete, his breath coming in gasps. By pushing his body from right to left he knew he was building up more speed than usual, and the panic rose from the pit of his stomach as he soared up the ramp, launched off, bent down, grabbed the bottom of the deck, let go – and just failed to make contact with the other side. He fell sideways, bashing his shoulder on the raw concrete, feeling his skin burn, and then landing upside down in a sea of stinking litter.

Rik lay there for a few seconds, wondering what he had broken. Then he moved gingerly and discovered that although his shoulder was smarting he seemed to be intact. He had always been good at gym at school and knew instinctively how to fall,

and of course he was so light. Thankfully Rik
picked himself up and started all over again.

He stayed working at it for the next hour, but
every time he skated up the ramp his courage failed
him and he managed to stop himself at the brink,
poised on his deck on the narrow ledge, staring

down at the abyss below him in horror. Then, using every last ounce of courage he had left, Rik got up speed again and on reaching the top, bent down without grabbing the deck and took off into the air. This time he crashed down on his feet, his deck following him, clunking him painfully on the head as it crashed to the ground. Trembling, jarred, sweating and virtually in tears, Rik stood in the filthy gully, looking up at the high, bleak sides of concrete above him, feeling angry and defeated.

Later, Rik walked over to Casey Jones at Waterloo station and using his school dinner money bought himself a bag of chips and a small orangeade. That completely cleaned him out and he felt very depressed as he walked back to the South Bank. His father's words echoed in his head, he had not yet got anywhere near mastering the jump and he could imagine his parents coming home from work, petting Helen and forgetting all about him.

'He'll come home when it suits him,' he could hear his mother saying, while his father added censoriously, 'That boy needs a good hiding – and he'll get it!'

Throughout the afternoon Rik continued to practise, but his nerve had now gone completely and he could only skate up the ramp – and roll miserably back. By four he was feeling exhausted, and by five sick and terribly hungry. His stomach rumbled and his head felt muzzy, yet Rik kept trying, going up the ramp time after time – and still rolling back. By half past five he thought he was going to faint and his whole body ran with a sticky sweat, but by six he had a second wind and he felt stronger both physically and mentally.

It was getting cold now and shadows moved underneath the walkways as the homeless clambered into sleeping bags if they were lucky and under newspapers and cardboard if they weren't. I'll be sleeping with this lot tonight, thought Rik – at least, I will be if I don't make the jump. I'll never make it, he thought gloomily and with mounting desperation, never ever make it. He looked round again at the dim figures settling into Cardboard City and wondered if they'd be friendly to be with or whether they would chuck him out just like his dad had done. Why don't they come and find me, thought Rik suddenly and the tears pricked at the back of his eyes. He might as well have been back in the children's home, feeling unwanted and uncared for.

Parents – they were all the same: hostile and unreliable – they'd desert you in the end. A tear trickled down Rik's grubby cheek and then another, but he brushed them away angrily, a renewed determination coming over him. He'd crack that jump by the time the light faded or die in the attempt.

A few other skaters had turned up and he tried to look cool and not exhausted in front of them. They gave him the impetus to summon up more courage or be shown up, and he went up the ramp even faster than he had done before, a new recklessness coming over him. This time he yanked the deck on to the ramp with his legs and at least half of it hit the concrete across the chasm. But it wasn't enough, and he fell backwards into the stinking pit and hit his head on an abandoned wooden box. It was this that saved him from serious injury; otherwise his head would have been cracked open on the unyield-ing concrete.

Rik struggled to his feet, dazed and shocked, but no-one came up to him or even sympathized with his fall. The skaters just continued their railslides and 180s and 360s and grabs and moves, although no-one, he noticed, attempted the jump. Rik stood there, gazing at them bleakly and then returned to his old cycle of dashing up the ramp and pulling back at the last moment. This seemed to last an eternity until Rik's second wind started running out and he knew it was hopeless, that he'd never succeed in mastering the jump before dark. Still determined not to go home and admit defeat, he felt sick and afraid, knowing he would have to face hours in Cardboard City before first light.

Gradually, as the shadows lengthened, the other skaters went away and Rik was alone again, still trying, but still holding back at the edge while the sweat ran into his eyes, continually blinding him. He realized that by now he must stink as much as the pit he was trying to cross, but he didn't care. Again he got his deck at high speed, again he went up the ramp, again he faltered at the brink.

Then he saw them, standing in a half circle in the gloom. His own desperate concentration and the hooting of boats on the river must have concealed the sound of their arrival. They had closely-shaved heads, gaudy clothes, chains, tight torn jeans and were wearing roller-boots. All were about sixteen; all were grinning and mocking him.

'We been watching you,' said one of the gang who had a spike through his nose. 'What you doing then?'

'It doesn't matter.'

'Come on!'

'Just skating.'

'Why do you keep going up that ramp? You're

not getting anywhere,' said another with a bright orange scarf in his hair.

'I'm all right.'

'You a nutter?' asked a third. They began to move in and the one with the spike through his nose took off his roller-boots and walked over to Rik.

'Let's have a go.'

Rik picked up his deck and backed up against a pillar.

'Come on.'

'I don't let anyone on my deck.'

'But you'll let me.' He was very close now and Rik knew he was in dead trouble.

'No,' he said defiantly.

'That's not nice.'

The rest of the gang were grinning away now.

'I said – no.'

'Let's have it.'

'Get lost!'

'He's not nice, is he?' said the boy, turning round to his audience who moved in still further. 'Not nice at all. Now give it here.'

'No way.' Rik was almost crushed into the concrete now, his deck hugged to his chest.

'Hang on!'

Someone stepped out of the shadows – and then someone else. They were big men, in their thirties, dressed in sweat shirts and jeans with tattoos running down the rippling muscles of their arms. One had a beard, the other, slightly younger, was clean shaven, and it was he who was doing the talking.

'What's going on?'

'Nothing,' said the roller-booter with the spike through his nose.

'You having a go at this kid?'

'No.'

'I think you are.'

'Only asked him if I could have a go on his deck.'

'Can't you take a hint? He doesn't want you to, does he? Look – he's practically disappearing into the concrete.'

'I only asked—'

'Yeah. Now clear off!'

Both the big men advanced on the roller-booters who began to back off. Hastily, the boy with the spike through his nose put his roller-boots back on.

'All right. All right.'

'Move!'

'We're going.'

They turned tail and rollered away, making sure they cheered and catcalled from a safe distance. Then they were gone.

'You look all in, kid,' said the younger of the tattooed men. 'And relax, we're not gonna take your board. We were watching you trying your jump. It'll come off one day. But you should go home now. It gets dodgy round here late at night.'

'Can't go home,' said Rik, emerging from his pillar.

'Why not?' asked the older man. He spoke with a gravelly voice and didn't seem to be so friendly. 'You shouldn't be around here on your own.'

'Gotta get this right first.'

'Hoppit.'

'Wait a minute.' The younger man eyed him curiously. 'Why is it so important?'

'Just is.'

'And you can't go home till it's done?'

'No.'

'I was like you as a kid. Persistent. My name's Harry. This is my mate Dennis. We're not going to stay long – and you shouldn't really be talking to us, not to strangers like – so I'm gonna give you a piece of advice and then clear off. Right?'

Rik stared at them, still clutching his skateboard, as wary of them now as he had been of the rollerbooters. Suddenly he nodded and said, 'What's your advice then?'

'My kid brother tries jumps like this, real hard

ones, and he always takes his deck a long way back. His trick is – more speed and a hard shove before he goes over. That's how he does it. So why don't you give it a try?'

Rik hesitated. Harry made it all sound so easy. His kid brother came across as a right little know-all, and yet—

'Go on, the longer run gives you more speed, and as you come off the ramp let the deck do the work. That should do it.' Harry's voice was warm and enthusiastic, willing Rik to do it, and his enthusiasm was catching. 'Why don't you give it a whirl?'

'Yes,' said Rik reluctantly.

'One other thing you need to do, kid.' Dennis suddenly came to life and for once he didn't sound mocking. 'Believe in yourself.' He laughed harshly but his eyes were as warm and encouraging as Harry's. 'Go for it, kid. Remember what he said – and go. Now. Before you change your mind.'

Rik took his skateboard as far back as he could. Then he went for it, feeling the others' confidence almost as if it was inside him, like a warm glow that was willing him on. He had never travelled so fast on his deck before and he hit the ramp with tremendous speed. But despite this his head remained cool and calm and he did exactly what Harry had told him to do and, when he came to the edge of the abyss, letting the deck do all the work, it zoomed across the gap, striking the concrete fair and square, well away from the edge. He'd done it. He was amazed – but he'd done it.

A burst of applause came not only from Harry and Dennis but from dozens of people he couldn't see, crouched in their newspapers and cardboard and bedding.

'I did it, Harry,' yelled Rik.

'Sure you did.' Harry was very laid back. 'Now come round here and do it again. Prove it wasn't a one-off.'

Grinning, Rik came back and did as he was told.

In all Rik successfully made the jump five times, and he gathered more confidence each time, despite the fact that it was nearly dark. It was on the sixth that he noticed a little group of spectators had built up on the river walk – and standing at the back of them was a familiar figure. It was his dad. When he saw that Rik had seen him he came slowly forward.

'Dad!'

He looked very haggard as he grabbed Rik by the shoulder. Harry and Dennis grinned and walked slowly away.

'Where've you been? I've looked all over. I've been to every skateboard park—'

'Did you see what I did? It was the jump I couldn't do. I did it, Dad!'

His father took no notice. 'Do you realize how worried me and your mother have been? Anything could have happened to you.'

'I've been practising all day,' said Rik who was hardly listening. 'Then these blokes showed me.' He turned round but saw they'd gone. 'Watch me now.'

But his father put out a restraining hand as Rik

prepared to go into action for the seventh time. 'You're coming home.'

'Am I in trouble?'

He paused and then said slowly, 'It's our fault – just as much as yours.'

'Wish Mum could see me do the jump.'

His father suddenly grinned. 'She will and all.'

'When?' Rik was suspicious.

'Tomorrow morning. We'll all take the day off.'

'What?'

'I'll drive the whole lot of you up here so you can show that jump to me and Mum and Helen. Would you like that?'

'Yeah!'

'Come on then.'

Rik stared into the darkness of Cardboard City. A little wind rattled the litter and sent a Coke can rolling and clattering on the pavement. Rik looked at the jump confidently; he knew he could do it again.

WHAT'S IN A NAME?

by Mary Ross

Roz glared at her mother. 'There's not even a decent ice-rink,' she stormed. 'What about all the competitions and things? I'll never be able to enter them now we're here.'

Mrs Tompkin looked up from the newspaper. 'Don't keep on, Roz. What did you expect us to do – stay in London and let your father live in digs?'

'He could have turned it down,' she muttered beneath her breath.

'Give up, kid.' Her brother gave her a warning glance. 'Mum and Dad have got enough to worry about without you wittering on all the time.'

Roz subsided into sulky silence. It's all right for Tony, she thought. He's away at college. It's me that has to live here.

Yesterday had been her first day at the new school, and it had been awful. Absolutely foul. She had got lost about a million times, and every time she went to sit down somebody would say, 'Sorry, I'm keeping that for Gillian,' or Debbie, or some other stuck-up pig. And as for the teachers!

'Name please,' the form teacher had said.

'Roz. Roz Tompkin.'

'Roz? How do you spell it?'

'R . . . O . . . Z.'

'Is that your full name?'

All eyes were on her. She felt herself going red. 'It's short for Rosanne,' she said, 'but everyone calls me Roz.'

'Do they indeed?'

'Yes, they do,' she said defiantly.

The teacher looked up sharply, her lips tightening. For a moment Roz thought she had gone too far. But then the teacher looked back down at the register and the moment had passed.

A girl in the front row turned round, her eyes hard as burnt currants. Her mouth curved in a knowing smirk, and Roz saw her nudge the girl next to her.

At break, a group of them gathered round her. 'Hey, what's your name?' Burnt currants asked. 'What's the A stand for?'

'The A?' Startled, Roz swung round to face her.

'It's on a name tag, sticking out of the back of your shirt. R. A. Tompkin. What you got a name tag for? Couldn't you remember your own name?'

Roz flushed painfully. She'd been a weekly boarder at the other school and everything had to be labelled. Why hadn't she remembered to cut it off?

'R. A. Tompkin,' Burnt currants said again. 'You know what that spells? RAT!'

Suddenly they formed a circle round her, chanting, 'Ratty, Ratty. She's going batty.'

Nearer and nearer they came, menacing her with leering faces. Roz bit her lip. There was no way she'd tell them what the A stood for. Maybe she could force her way out of the circle? Hit one of them in the teeth? Kick her way out? She clenched her fist in readiness . . .

Dring . . . dring. The shrill note of the school bell cut through her thoughts and the circle drifted away like magic as everyone crowded towards the doors.

A slim Asian girl smiled at her as they walked back into the classroom. 'Don't worry about Louise,' she whispered. 'She's like this with all the new girls.'

After lunch there was a note on the register. Puzzled, the teacher read it. 'Does anyone know anything about this?' she enquired, holding it up.

'No Miss Jenkyns,' the class chorused.

The teacher sighed. 'Stand up Rosanne,' she said.

Thirty pairs of eyes swivelled round to look at her.

Miss Jenkyns paused. She knew exactly how long to time it for the most effect. Taking off her spectacles, she put them carefully down on the register. 'I thought I asked you this morning what was your full name. Perhaps I forgot? Or perhaps you didn't hear me?'

The silence seemed to go on for ever.

'Well?'

'I heard you, miss.'

It was like a cat playing with a mouse. The voice was still silky smooth. 'Perhaps you didn't understand. Would anyone like to explain what "full name" means?'

A hand shot up in the air. Roz didn't need to look. She knew exactly whose hand it was.

'Please, miss.' The hand waggled importantly.

'Ah. I thought it might be you, Louise.'

'Full name means the complete name . . . all of it . . .' The voice gloated in its power.

'Thank you.' The teacher's gaze returned to her victim. 'Now, would you please give me your full name – including your middle name.'

'Rosanne Andrianov Tompkin.'

The explosion of laughter was quickly stifled as the teacher tapped her pen on the desk. 'Enough! Andrianov? How do you spell it?'

Roz told her.

'In future, when I ask a question I expect a truthful answer. Understand?'

Roz nodded miserably.

'And Louise?'

'Yes, miss?' Louise glowed with triumph.

'If I need help with my register or anything else, I will ask for it. Is that understood?'

Louise glared at Roz before lowering her eyes. 'Yes, miss.'

When she got home Roz flung her bag down in a corner and slammed the front door. 'Was it that bad?' She felt her mother's hand on her shoulder.

'Yes it was,' she fumed. 'They called me Ratty again. Just like they did in the last school.'

Her mother tried to put an arm round her, but Roz shrugged it away. There was a pause, then her mother said gently, 'Your father went back to Richmond today – to the ice-rink. He's arranged for you to take up your ice-skating lessons again. It's only an hour on the motorway, so I'll be able to take you in the car most times. If I can't you'll have to go by train. It'll mean getting up very early on Mondays and Fridays – but I don't suppose you'll mind?'

Anger forgotten, Roz flung her arms round her mother. 'Brilliant. Thanks, Mum. That'll be great.'

After that first week the new school didn't seem so bad. Roz made a few friends and now that she was back ice-skating nothing else mattered. Louise soon found someone else to bully and left her alone – though the nickname stuck, worse luck.

'You were lucky,' her new friend, Sula, said. 'Last year, on Sports Day, Louise and a couple of her pals were going to beat me up after school just because I was faster than her in the one hundred metres race.'

Roz stared at her. 'And did she?'

Sula shook her head. 'No fear. I came second in the next race. I'm not stupid.'

'You mean you ducked it, just because Louise threatened you?'

Sula flushed. 'What else could I do?'

'But surely if the rest of you stuck together?' Her voice trailed away. What was the use? If nobody had managed to get their own back up to now, what chance would she have?

They were practising hard at Richmond for the Inter-club Competitions. Roz knew that she had a good chance of winning her section in the free skating, and she was looking forward to it, but she was looking forward even more to what came after . . . The last part of the programme was a show skating exhibition by the home team, and she and

Tony had worked out a clown routine that had the rest of them in stitches.

'Honestly, it's brilliant,' she told Sula. 'I didn't think Tony would be able to take part this year – with going to college and everything, but it's only a bus ride away so I've seen more of him this term than I did when we were *living* in London.'

.She didn't tell any of the others about her ice-skating. Well, if Louise and her lot heard about it they'd make her life a misery, wouldn't they? But then Miss Jenkyns, the form teacher, said that they would be going up to Richmond to watch the competitions . . .

'A coach will pick us up outside the school gates at ten o'clock,' Miss Jenkyns said. 'I'm told that Louise is one of our most promising skaters. I hope that as many of you as possible will support her.'

On Thursday, Miss Jenkyns collected the money from those who were going on the trip. When she got to the T's in the register she paused.

'Rosanne Tompkin?' She had never got round to calling her Roz, but at least nobody laughed at it any more.

'No, miss,' Roz stammered. 'That is, yes, miss. But I'm going with my mum in the car. I'm in them.'

'In the competitions?'

Everyone's eyes were on her. 'Yes miss, I go skating twice a week – before I come to school.'

The teacher's eyes were reflective. She looked as though she were searching her memory for something . . . 'I see. Well, this will make it even more interesting, won't it Louise?' But Louise only glared.

The class were already taking up most of the front row and talking excitedly, by the time Roz and her mother arrived. Sula looked round and waved, but no-one else seemed to notice her. For the first time she felt self-conscious. Don't let anything go wrong, she thought, crossing her fingers. Don't let me fall on that double axel. Not right at the beginning of the routine. It wouldn't matter so much on the combination . . . well, it would of course. But if she fell at the beginning it would put her off for the rest of the routine.

'Is that your class,' her mother asked. 'Aren't you going round to talk to them?'

'No. I feel embarrassed.'

'Embarrassed? I've never heard you say that before.' Her mother looked at her thoughtfully. 'You haven't told them, have you? Why not?'

Roz shrugged.

'Embarrassed about me? Because I used to be a famous skater?'

Roz felt a tell-tale blush spread up her neck.

At that moment they were called to warm up for the Free section, and she saw Louise take off her skate guards and thrust forward on to the ice. With thudding heart and tense muscles, Roz peeled off her anorak and followed her.

Louise was just taking off in a double toe loop when she saw Roz. For a split second she seemed to hang in the air before completely losing her balance and landing in an untidy heap on the ice. Grinning to herself, Roz skated past and into a three jump. As she landed she caught a glimpse of Louise's face.

'I'll get you, Ratty,' the girl hissed.

Roz giggled. 'You watch I don't get you first.'

The minute's warm-up sped past as she relaxed into the familiar spirals, jumps and arabesques. I wish I was on after Louise instead of before, she thought. There wasn't much chance to judge the other girl's standard when they were both skating. There would be no chance to see what Louise was like until after her own performance was finished.

'Clear the ice please.'

As she skated back to the barrier Roz noticed that her brother had arrived and was sitting next to her

mother. Good. Tony wasn't as critical of her skating as Mum was. Still, it was her mother's opinion she really valued.

A slight click signalled the beginning of the tape for the first competitor's music. Roz recognized the overture to *Aspects of Love*. It was a piece that she had nearly chosen herself. She was so glad now that she'd had second thoughts.

The music faded away leaving the skater in a

deep lunge, her arms draped over the forward leg. She stood up with look of relief on her face and skated back to the barrier.

After a pause the marks were called out. '3·5, 3·6, 3·2, 3·5.' Then for Artistic Impression. '3·4, 3·5, 3·4, 3·4.'

I can beat that, Roz thought.

Her throat was dry, and she fancied that everyone could hear the thudding of her heart as she took her position. One . . . Two . . . Three . . . Four. Music flooded the rink and she plunged into the complex routine of spins and jumps that her coach had choreographed to the music of *Carousel*. The fast section ended with a double axel and as she landed she heard a burst of applause. Then she glided into a spin as the musi changed to the slow sadness of *You'll Never Walk Alone*. Just listening to it gave her a lump in the throat, and the choreography with its long, graceful arm movements and slow arabesques mirrored her feelings.

Then she was into the last minute of the routine. The bouncy rhythm of the Clambake number jerked the audience into a fever of clapping in time to the music. They were so noisy that she nearly lost the last few bars, but somehow managed to catch the rhythm again just in time to dig in the left toe pick behind her, and fling her arms up on the very last note.

It was great. The best she'd ever done. Shaking with relief she skated across to the judges and curtsied, before going back to the barrier.

'For Technical Merit. 3·7, 3·8, 3·8, 3·8.'

Brilliant. She wiped her neck with the towel, taking in great gulps of air. Then came the next set of marks. 'Artistic Impression. 3·8, 3·9, 3·9, 3·8.' She heard a burst of applause, and was suddenly conscious of her form in the front row. They were still clapping her performance as Louise skated on to the ice to start her routine.

It wasn't a bad performance. She landed on two feet instead of one on her first jump, but other than that not bad at all. But she seemed to have lost the will to win. It was as if she were on automatic pilot. As if she had given up before she had really started. And the marks reflected that. One 3·5. That was the highest mark she got.

The last girl in the section was hopeless. She slipped and fell halfway through her routine and went to pieces after that. No contest there. Roz was the clear winner, and as she went up to receive her medal, she saw her mother smiling proudly from the crowd.

In the break, the Polar Bear Ice machine lumbered on to the ice to get it ready for the show skating exhibition that was to follow. Roz saw Sula weaving her way through the skaters towards her. 'That was fantastic!' she gasped. 'I never thought you were that good. Miss Jenkyns is really stunned. Come and talk.'

'I can't. I've got to get changed. We're doing a circus scene, and Tony and I are the clowns.'

'Is that your brother?' Sula asked, gazing past her towards the seats where her mother and Tony were sitting.

'Yeah.'

'He doesn't look a bit like you. You're so dark.'

'I follow my mum. She's from Russia.'

Sula blinked. 'You're a cool one, Ratty. You never tell me anything.'

Roz grinned. 'Well I am telling you now. Anyway, I must go and change.'

With ginger wigs and comic makeup, Tony and Roz were waiting behind the barrier at the far end of the rink as the lights dimmed for the circus scene.

Roz's nervousness had completely disappeared. This would be fun, she thought. They had worked on the routine so often she could do it with her eyes shut. She studied the audience carefully. Yes, it couldn't have been better. Miss Jenkyns and the rest of the class would have a real eyeful.

The brassy overture faded, and the DJ's voice crackled out over the microphone. 'Our first number in this section of the programme is, "Entry of the Clowns", with Tony and Rosanne Tompkin. The mums and dads in the audience will perhaps remember Rosanne Andrianov – the champion Russian skater who took the gold medal three years running in the 1970's? Well Tony and Roz are her children, so a big welcome please to . . . *Tony and Rosanne Tompkin.*'

It was a crazy routine – simple but effective – in which they soaked each other with bucket after bucket of water. Every so often one would stagger towards the audience as if they were going to pour the water over them, then skilfully spin round so that the water dashed harmlessly on to the ice.

The music was coming to a climax. Roz skated across to the barrier to refill her bucket – only this time from the other container.

She zig-zagged jerkily towards where the class were sitting, acting as if he bucket was so heavy that it would trip her up at any moment. Sula and the others were laughing and giggling like crazy, and even Miss Jenkyns looked amused.

Miss Jenkyns and Louise were sitting at the end

of the row. Roz paused, then spun round to face them, swinging the bucket in time to the music.

'Shall I?' she asked the audience.

'Yes!' The answer came back in a roar.

'One . . .'

'Two,' they yelled delightedly.

'*Three!*' In one swift movement she tossed the contents of the bucket towards them, then went skating away behind the curtains at the far end of the barrier.

Louise screamed hysterically. She hardly seemed to notice that the frothy white torrent that shot from the bucket was not the ice-cold water that they had been expecting – but a flurry of feathers. And even when she did, she just sat there open mouthed . . . one curly white feather quivering gently on her upper lip.

The rest of the form went wild. 'Serves you right,' someone shouted. Then they all began to chant . . .

'Ratty. Ratty. We want Ratty!' The rest of the audience took it up. 'Ratty. Ratty. We want Ratty.'

Roz and her brother skated out into the spotlight to take their bow. She glanced towards the row where her form were sitting, and her eyes widened with surprise. Louise had disappeared, but Miss Jenkyns was still there – brushing off the feathers and chanting with the rest.

'Ratty. Ratty. We want Ratty.' Not Rosanne. Or even Roz. But Ratty. And everyone was smiling. As if they really liked her.

Roz grinned. Suddenly the hated nickname didn't seem so bad after all.

LEFT FOOT FORWARD

by Jan Mark

Singlewell High School was small, but St George's C of E Primary had been even smaller. Waiting for his first PE lesson, feeling dwarfish in the high green vaults of the Singlewell changing room, Shaun remembered St George's and felt almost homesick.

In the doorway Mr Durkin loomed. Mr Durkin taught PE and games, and nothing else. At St George's Mrs Calloway had taken them for everything; maths and language, science, cookery, music, art – and football. There were so few of them that to get a team together they used to amalgamate with the boys from Church Whitton and even then Emily Stowe had to be goalie.

Emily was away with the girls now, mutinously playing netball. On the bus home, after the first day at Singlewell, Emily had confided to Shaun that she was going to ask Mr Durkin if she could go on with football, but Shaun, now eyeing Mr Durkin's silhouette, doubted that she would get much encouragement. Mr Durkin reminded Shaun of something out of a horror movie; not the old-fashioned kind where a mad scientist, holed up in a derelict Bavarian schloss, created an uncontrollable monster, but the type that turned up on video featuring cybernetic mutants from the future, computerized and ruthless. Seen in that light, Mr Durkin was state of the art.

By the end of the lesson, Shaun realized that he had got it all wrong. Mr Durkin was large but mild. It was Mr Prior, his sidekick, half the size but twice as noisy, who supplied the sound and the fury. Ian Edwards, from Church Whitton, remarked that Durkin and Prior were really an interrogation team, taking turns to soften you up and then rough you up. Ian did not care either way. He was sure of a place in any team going.

Mr Durkin stayed very much in the background while Mr Prior conducted the lesson with a series of barks and grunts. Mr Durkin was watchful; he was on the look-out.

Talent scout, Shaun thought; he's *noticing* people. Ian was noticed, and Tom Carter who had come to Singlewell with Shaun, from St George's. Shaun was noticed too, but in a different way. This became apparent the following Monday, when they had their first games lesson. Sides were chosen. Unlike St George's there were enough of them in the first year for two teams. Shaun was not in either. Mr Prior growled something about acquiring ball skills and sent him, with three other rejects, to kick about on a disused pitch that sloped and had outcrops of rock in it.

'We're the ones with two left feet,' said Edgar Crump, cheerfully, and acquired rock skills, while the other three deployed their six left feet with a mildewed ball that leaked air and, mysteriously, bubbles of moisture. Mr Durkin passed once in their direction, cried, 'That's right; keep it up, lads,' and swerved away again. Shaun, changing afterwards, foresaw that the rest of the term, the rest of the year, possibly the rest of his life was going to be spent like that. Edgar did not mind. He was prepared to wait until May, when his fast bowling would be revealed to the unsuspecting Prior and Durkin. The other two left-footers planned to bring along computer games next time. As far as they were concerned, Monday football constituted an extended lunch hour.

Shaun consulted his timetable and discovered that Monday afternoon was scheduled to end as badly as it had begun. The next lesson was double maths. On his last day at St George's Mrs Calloway had taken him aside and said, 'Don't worry about going to big school. You'll get on fine – but you'll have to work hard at your maths. Promise me you'll do that.'

Shaun had promised. He meant to keep his word and for the first ten minutes of the lesson he paid careful attention, sitting upright with his arms folded upon his new file, with its single sheet of paper on which he had written the date and under-lined it neatly. But gradually, like drizzle, a grey memory fell before his eyes; the steep and stony pitch, the flabby ball, the clumsy rejected boots of the eight left feet; new boots, in his case. It did not matter about the others. They didn't care what they played, but he had been looking forward to the games lesson. He loved football. He hated maths. It was going to be a real effort to keep his promise to Mrs Calloway, but he loved football. It had never mattered that the combined team of St George's and Church Whitton had not won a match in three seasons; he enjoyed playing.

The next games period found the eight left feet back on the pitch of stones. Alongside them, on the real pitch, the rest of the group played a real game, while beyond that rose occasional shrieks as Emily Stowe put the fear of God into the netball players.

Edgar had joined the computer freaks, so Shaun had sole possession of the ball, which was no longer round but lopsided, like the gibbous moon.

He dribbled it up and down the pitch, pirouetting round flints and tussocks and the strange scaly leaves that sprouted in clumps, alien vegetation from a distant planet. The phantom figures of twenty-one players surrounded him, but he eluded

them all, scoring goal after goal. Phantom goalies flung themselves at his headers in futile dives. Phantom team mates hugged him. Occasionally he glanced round to see if Mr Prior or Mr Durkin were looking his way. They never were.

On the way back to the changing room a row broke out. Mr Prior had been particularly noisy at close of play. 'Hark at him,' muttered a gingery boy from 1g. 'Anyone would think we were at Wembley. It's only a game.'

A fiery glow seemed to envelop Mr Prior. *'Only a game?* I can't be bothered with people who aren't prepared to give one hundred per cent and then some extra. Only a game? If that's how you feel you can go and play hopscotch. I'm sure we can find someone to take your place.'

Shaun's excitement punched him in the ribs. If they were looking for someone else to take the place of the gingery boy from 1g, there was only one other place where they could look. The same thought occurred to Mr Prior.

'So watch it,' he added lamely.

If only maths did not come next. If only the bad times did not have to happen on Monday afternoons, infecting everything that followed during the rest of the week. English was his best subject; art was fun; geography was easy. He had all three on Monday mornings, a wonderful start to the week. Kind words rang in his ears; complimentary red comments underlined his homework; a sketch of Edgar's feet, which he had knocked off in twenty minutes, ascended miraculously to a place on the wall beside some sixth-former's A level life study. By lunchtime he ought to have been buoyant, confident, set up for success, but the praise was hollow. Beneath the buoyancy lay a dark despondent pit. His self esteem leaked damply away. *After* lunch there was nothing to look forward to but that dismal hour on the pitch of stones, followed by a more dismal hour of maths.

Today was misty. The school, lying on a hillside above the estuary, was swept by coastal squalls, off-shore winds and sea fog. The wet air thickened, white and heavy. The farther goal vanished in the pallid murk; the adjacent pitch was invisible, although Shaun could tell how the game was going by the surge of noise, ebbing and flowing tidally in the fog; stampeding feet, the thud of boot on ball, the duetting whistles of Prior and Durkin, now close at hand, now fading eerily. Mainly the sounds were at the upper end of the pitch and his heart went out to the lonely goalie on the winning side, marooned in his net at the lower end where he waited for the ball to emerge from the vapour.

After that, the first five minutes of the maths lesson were almost enjoyable. All the lights were on, the radiators were hot. Shaun snuggled down in his corner seat and thawed contentedly, but it could not last. Homework was being handed back. Little was said, but people were looking congratulations at each other as Miss Stevens prowled the classroom, doling out sheets of paper.

'Just proving she knows our names already,' said Ian in front, over his shoulder. 'Show-off.'

'I knew *yours* on the first day,' Miss Stevens said, slapping down his paper in front of him. 'We always notice the loudmouths first. Well done, anyway.'

Ian grinned and turned to pick up his paper. Shaun saw the short hairs on the back of his neck bristle with pride – but now it was Shaun's turn, the last paper of all, limp and forlorn. Shaun looked up at its underside and recognized one of his own dirty thumb prints between Miss Stevens's clean fingertips.

'You don't really seem to have got the hang of this,' Miss Stevens said, laying the paper on his desk so that he could see all the red writing, none of it complimentary this time, that covered it. 'I'll have a word with you at the end of the lesson.'

'Have you always found maths difficult?' Miss Stevens asked, at the end of the lesson.

Shaun nodded, although it was not strictly true. Years ago it had seemed as easy as anything else, in the infants, when it was just something that he did, in those days before it sneakily detached itself from the rest of his education and became maths. But Miss Stevens had BSc. after her name and would not know about the infants.

'Yes, miss,' he said.

Miss Stevens looked kind; sad, but kind. 'I suppose you're one of the bus people.'

He could not see what that had to do with it; whizz-kid Ian was a bus person and it did not seem to do his maths any harm. What he could see, out in the fog, were the headlights of the bus itself, and he had about three minutes in which to catch it.

'Yes, miss.'

'Well then, I can't suggest that you stop after school for extra tuition – some people do that. But you do need help. Are you in the band – or gym club?'

'No, miss.' She certainly did know how to stray off the subject.

'Then you'd better come along to my room tomorrow lunchtime. We'll see how that goes for a few weeks, shall we?'

She was doing him a favour, he knew that. He made a grateful noise and backed out of the room, racing for the cloakroom and then the bus, where Emily Stowe was cock-a-hoop, running up and down the gangway and punching the air. She had been sent off, during netball. No-one in the history of the school, she thought, had ever had a red card in netball.

'It wasn't a foul, though,' she explained, settling next to Shaun as the bus started. 'I'd never do nothing like that. I just throw the ball too hard and no-one can't catch it. They fall over.'

She tried to sound remorseful, but Shaun could envision the other netball players, felled like skittles by Emily's demon delivery.

'I've got to do extra maths,' Shaun said.

'What, for homework?' Emily said. 'I'll help. I'll do it for you.' She had done a lot of it for him at St George's, too. That had been part of the trouble.

'No, at school, Tuesday lunchtime,' Shaun said and saw, with sinking spirits, how the awfulness of Monday was spilling over into Tuesday; how soon, like a creeping paralysis, it would take over Wednesday, and Thursday too, until it ruined the whole week.

When, on the following Monday, Shaun looked at the classroom calendar before registration, he realized that there were only two weeks left before half term. He had heard somewhere that time passes more quickly as you get older. His life was skidding away from under him, and he knew why. At St George's he had taken one day at a time because, except for birthdays and Christmas, or bad moments due to his own villainy, one day had been as good as another. But now he spent his time wishing that Monday was over, even as early as the previous Tuesday. Life had been reduced to a series of Mondays; he scarcely noticed what came in between.

It was a frosty day, clear and bright. From the pitch of stones he could see the estuary glinting in the distance. Weak but well-intentioned sunlight gilded the smoke stacks on the cement works. It was too cold to stand about so the other left feet abandoned the computer games and joined Shaun with the bad-news ball; not the original one which had collapsed altogether and gone strangely stiff, but a replacement, equally limp and soggy. Shaun suspected that somewhere there was a factory turning out special partially-collapsed footballs for people like him.

Indoors again, after they had changed, Mr Durkin read out a list of names. Mr Prior stood by, casting a watchful eye over them.

'All these boys,' he said, 'will report here for extra coaching on Wednesday lunchtimes.' Shaun mentally reviewed the list. Ian Edwards and Tom Carter were on it, even the gingery boy from 1g. Edgar Crump was not, nor was Shaun, nor any of the other left feet. Those who *were* on it smiled at each other.

'What's them two so pleased with themselves about?' asked Emily Stowe, later, on the bus, as Tom and Ian toasted each other in Seven-Up.

'They've been picked for extra football,' Shaun said.

'I'm going to be let do hockey after half term,' Emily said, 'with the second years.' She paused and thought. 'Why're they doing extra football?'

'Because they're good at it,' Shaun said. 'For the team.'

'But that's not why you get extra maths, is it?' Emily said. 'You get extra maths because you're *not* good at it.'

Shaun felt his gloom pierced by a needle of resentment.

'Yes,' he said.

'Well that's not fair is it?' Emily said. 'You get extra maths because you *can't* do it, and they get extra football because they *can*.'

Shaun's needle became a bodkin, then a six-inch nail.

'If I was you,' Emily advised, with an evil smile,

'I'd ask old Durkin if you can have extra football too.'

He knew that she was not really concerned on his behalf. He had once heard Mrs Calloway describe Emily Stowe as a stirrer. She was stirring now. She liked the idea of a fight.

'You ask him, on Wednesday,' she said. 'I'll come with you.'

Shaun thought that this last was the least attractive proposition he had heard in a long while. But the one before it had certain possibilities.

'I'll ask him by myself,' he said.

'I'll watch,' said Emily.

Tuesday's extra maths tuition was not a success. Shaun's mind was on other things. On Wednesday, with Emily at a constant but safe distance, he went along to the changing room, carrying his kit.

Mr Durkin never changed, nor Mr Prior. They seemed to live in their tracksuits, appearing in them for games and PE, at registration and assembly, Mr Prior's small and purple, Mr Durkin's large and black. Shaun approached the large black tracksuit.

'Sir?'

'Now, what do you want?' Mr Durkin asked. 'This is extra coaching time.'

'Yes,' Shaun said. 'I know. I want to do extra coaching.'

'No, no,' said Mr Durkin, good-humouredly, as if explaining to an idiot something very obvious, such as how button-holes work. 'This is for the boys who will be in the team.'

'Yes. I want to be in the team,' Shaun said.

He could see Mr Durkin's problem. If Shaun went on like this Mr Durkin would be forced to say, out loud that Shaun had two left feet and might just as well be applying to join the England squad. Out of the corner of his eye he could also see, through the frosted glass panel of the door, Emily Stowe, eavesdropping, longing to rush in and speak up for him. He had to speak up for himself before Emily burst through the door (not bothering to open it but leaving an Emily-shaped hole in the glass, like Desperate Dan) and gazed unblushingly at Ian Edwards and Tom Carter with no trousers on.

'Look, sir,' said Shaun, 'I have to do extra maths with Miss Stevens so I can get good at it. I want to get good at football. I want to do extra, like the others.'

Mr Prior, at this point, might have exploded and seriously damaged Shaun in the blast, but Mr Durkin, fatally, gave himself time to think.

'I'm never going to get good if I don't practise, am I, sir?' Shaun said.

'No-one is stopping you from practising,' Mr Durkin said.

'I can't practise on my own,' Shaun persisted, 'not on that horrible old pitch with that horrible old ball. Not with people who don't care anyway. I want to play properly. I don't see why I shouldn't do it at all just because I don't do it well. I mean—' he pressed home his advantage '—I mean, I couldn't go to Miss Stevens and say I wasn't going to do that extra maths 'cause I'm no good anyway, could I, sir?'

'That's a bit different,' Mr Durkin said. 'Maths is important. After all, football's only—'

He stopped. He did not say it. Just in time he saw the trap, and it was his own mouth. Then he looked round and saw Mr Prior. Shaun fancied that he detected a light sweat breaking out on Mr Durkin's forehead.

'What's this lad up to?' Mr Prior asked. 'Giving trouble?'

'Not at all,' said Mr Durkin. 'He's just come along to watch the coaching. I think,' said Mr Durkin, and Shaun could see him thinking, 'that shows real enthusiasm, don't you?'

'Yes!' cried Mr Prior, with no enthusiasm at all.

He wheeled, and bolted back to the players. 'Come on, boys. Outside in five seconds flat!'

'Enthusiasm . . . important attitude . . . essential to team spirit . . .'. Mr Durkin was chuntering. 'Remind me at the start of the lesson next Monday. I'll see that you get a game – time we tried out some of you others . . . oh.' He hesitated. 'I suppose there's no chance that the rest think as you do?' Shaun smiled kindly.

208

'What, Edgar and that? Oh no, sir, just me . . . I think,' he added, and had the satisfaction of seeing Mr Durkin cringe at the prospect of Edgar and the other left feet taking steps to improve their game.